Religion and Science Fiction

Images of Elsewhere

Vol. II

PETER LANG
Oxford - Berlin - Bruxelles - Chennai - Lausanne - New York

Religion and Science Fiction

Timothy Jenkins

PETER LANG
Oxford · Berlin · Bruxelles · Chennai · Lausanne · New York

Bibliographic information published by the Deutsche Nationalbibliothek.
The German National Library lists this publication in the German National Bibliography;
detailed bibliographic data is available on the Internet at http://dnb.d-nb.de.

A catalogue record for this book is available from the British Library.

Library of Congress Cataloging-in-Publication Data

Names: Jenkins, Timothy, 1952- author.
Title: Religion and science fiction. Vol. II, : Images of elsewhere /
   Timothy Jenkins.
Other titles: Images of elsewhere
Description: Oxford ; New York : Peter Lang Publishing, 2025. | Includes
   bibliographical references and index.
Identifiers: LCCN 2024035336 (print) | LCCN 2024035337 (ebook) |
   ISBN 9781803741703 (paperback) | ISBN 9781803741710 (ebook) |
   ISBN 9781803741727 (epub)
Subjects: LCSH: Unidentified flying objects—Religious aspects. |
   Unidentified flying objects in popular culture. | Theosophy in
   literature. | Theosophy in popular culture. | Science fiction—History
   and criticism. | American fiction—20th century_History and criticism.
   | LCGFT: Essays.
Classification: LCC BL65.U54 J46 2025 (print) | LCC BL65.U54 (ebook) |
   DDC 001.942—dc23/eng/20240812
LC record available at https://lccn.loc.gov/2024035336
LC ebook record available at https://lccn.loc.gov/2024035337

Cover image: Line drawing by the author.
Cover design by Peter Lang Group AG

ISBN 978-1-80374-170-3 (print)
ISBN 978-1-80374-171-0 (ePDF)
ISBN 978-1-80374-172-7 (ePub)
DOI 10.3726/b20808

© 2025 Peter Lang Group AG, Lausanne
Published by Peter Lang Ltd, Oxford, United Kingdom
info@peterlang.com - www.peterlang.com

Timothy Jenkins has asserted his right under the Copyright, Designs and Patents Act, 1988,
to be identified as Author of this Work.

All rights reserved.
All parts of this publication are protected by copyright.
Any utilisation outside the strict limits of the copyright law, without the permission of the
publisher, is forbidden and liable to prosecution.
This applies in particular to reproductions, translations, microfilming, and storage and processing
in electronic retrieval systems.

This publication has been peer reviewed.

Contents

Series Preface — vii

Introduction — 1

CHAPTER 1
An exemplary story in its setting — 3

CHAPTER 2
Theosophy, the source of this complex world picture — 33

CHAPTER 3
The 'Shaver Mystery' – sources and commentary — 75

Appendix: A study of Alfred Sinnett's *Esoteric Buddhism* (1883) — 99

Bibliography — 145

Index — 153

Series Preface

Reports of flying saucers – also known as UFOs – constitute a puzzle, for they are numerous, well attested, and hard to believe. There are tempting shortcuts to a 'solution' – that the sightings are real, or mistaken, or fictitious (made up) – but none of these prove satisfactory. Instead, we are brought to consider the history of sightings and the history, also, of how it became possible to regard such incidents in the terms that have become customary. Flying saucers in this fashion become a feature of the wider society, and allow an angle of approach to our modern, technological civilization: a small-scale problem that allows insight into the larger setting.

The six essays stand as independent studies. Each deals with an aspect of the life of flying saucers or UFOs: their appearance after the Second World War within the constellation of military and technological interests, their debt to early science fiction and its sources, the development of the search for signs of extra-terrestrial intelligence, the first adoptions of the 'interplanetary hypothesis' in civilian circles, the further expansion of reports, first, of sightings and, then, of abductions in the wider society, and, finally, a review of the range of forms which have appeared. Taken together, they form a thorough enquiry into reports of sightings of flying saucers.

The series as a whole makes three contributions to resolving the puzzle posed by such reports.

First, it relates three bodies of materials from the United States in the mid-twentieth century whose interactions must be taken into consideration when speaking about flying saucers. These are the science fiction milieu, the interplay of military and technical interests, and reports of sightings by members of the public; in short, stories, military work, and ordinary lives. The first contribution is to study their interactions, overlaps, borrowings and synergies.

The second is to derive the categories that are necessary to explain the convergence of these materials. Repeating patterns appear in science fiction literature, the history of Air Force intelligence in the Cold War period, the early days of NASA, the search for extra-terrestrial intelligence, and a wide variety of incidents and claims made by members of the public. To make sense of their common nature and to see how their interactions work, we also need to investigate some intellectual history. There is a longstanding tradition of popular thought putting new scientific discoveries and technological innovation to work for human moral purposes. This tradition was taken up by military and technical interests in the middle third of the twentieth century, using three clusters of ideas: the intimate connection between military technology and the world picture offered by modern media, the concept of 'communication' (and, post-War, of 'information') that became central in the period, and an understanding of 'memory' as an exact record of the past. These ideas were shared with a wider public: in the context of international tensions, hopes of communication and fears of its breakdown were given expression in the appearance of new forms of life, forms given content by the earlier longstanding history. This is the second contribution the essay makes to the topic: an investigation of the common patterns of thought necessary for stories, military work and ordinary lives to interact.

And, last, a mechanism is proposed by which these interactions occur. This is an analysis of the ways in which these 'images', which contain both real and imaginary elements, make their appearance compelling. I find well documented instances – in particular, the sessions in which memories of abductions are recovered – where the social mechanism is uncovered that allows the oscillation between the two elements, a mechanism that can be glimpsed at work in other sites but which cannot be tracked in such detail in the documents and other sources we have concerning advances in research, security decisions, the records of incidents and so forth. This is the third contribution.

I first came to the puzzle of flying saucer reports when working on spirit messages and similar forms of social life (such as parapsychology and psychical research) and realized that the search for extra-terrestrial intelligence was the latest expression of a long-held desire for communication with disembodied minds compatible with our own. It has taken a good deal of time and work to give substance to this insight. As will be clear from my references, there is an abundance of work of the highest quality

Series Preface

in this broad area, on which I draw to give shape to the argument. If I have contributed anything, it is by making a systematic enquiry and by putting together materials that are not always associated, and by continuing to ask questions rather than settling for accepted answers. In this fashion, I hope to have supported readers who find these topics interesting rather than those who wish to close them down, and I also hope to have contributed in some small degree to understanding the contemporary world.

Introduction

This essay is concerned with reading a single story drawn from 1940s pulp science fiction, together with exploring the images upon which it draws, which are to be found in the writings of a movement known as Theosophy. Investigating the story allows the tracing of a history whereby theosophical ideas became a resource for thinking and talking about the possibility of life elsewhere in the 1940s and 1950s.

I have two wider concerns which lie behind this choice of a story and exploration of its essential ideas. First, although there were earlier speculations about the possibility of life elsewhere in the Universe, they took a new form in the late nineteenth century. Theosophy was crucial for the formation of a particular notion, that of alien creatures which are interested in human life and, potentially, seek to aid our progress, linked themes that are central to our ideas of modern 'interplanetary' phenomena such as disks, flying saucers or UFOs. This notion was taken up and given independent expression in early forms of science fiction. Its wider importance was this: because of their focus on the contribution of scientific advances to understanding modern human potential – possible forms of human flourishing and of disaster – theosophical ideas could serve as a model for popular moral speculation in the context of the Second World War, their resources being transmitted through the pulp stories Theosophy had helped to shape. Identifying this source is not a claim about all science fiction, but it is a contribution to tracing the genealogy of the images which concern us. In this essay, to keep the focus tight, I have kept discussion of the implications of the claim for the wider genre brief, while at one point offering a list of authors who could be considered in this perspective.

The second concern is a broader claim about the nature of contemporary religion and the forms in which it is found in society, pointing to the contribution of what we might in shorthand call liberal Protestant thought to widespread practices of evaluation and intelligibility. In brief, we all draw on the resources of what is termed 'metaphysical religion', of which

Spiritualism and its off-shoot, Theosophy, are instances.[1] While, in contemporary historical and social scientific surveys, Spiritualism is sometimes attributed a marginal place when considering the locations where modern religion is found, I would suggest, on the contrary, that the categories and ways of reasoning it supports are to be found opportunistically at work in many places in the contemporary social order, including places dominated by technological, scientific, military and security concerns, but also in civil society where reparative and therapeutic ideas are invoked. So, while the focus is on the generation and history of flying saucer reports, in the background there is a recurring theme of the contribution of unproven ideas deriving from this metaphysical tradition to the creation and production of reliable knowledge, as well as the place of Theosophy in this tradition, particularly with respect to changing situations and innovation, and the role of science fiction in transmitting these ideas. Despite the restricted scope of the materials discussed in this essay, it contributes therefore in these two regards to the wider topic of the relations of religion and science fiction in the contemporary period.

---

1   William James makes the same point in *The Varieties of Religious Experience* (1902), drawing all his most telling examples from near-contemporary American metaphysical religion. For metaphysical religion as a topic, see Albanese (2007) and Bender (2010).

CHAPTER 1

An exemplary story in its setting

The appearance of flying saucers signals the construction of a new imaginative space, arising from the deployment of new weaponry and means of communication.[1] Under these conditions, we may ask from where comes the form to which modern technologies of various kinds give content and substance? With regard to flying saucers, this question comes down to asking what resources does science fiction, and pulp science fiction in particular, bring under these new conditions.

To answer this, I first describe a single story, published in 1945, which plays a particular role in the appearance of flying saucers. That role, however, was contingent; another story could have taken its place and, indeed, the entire genre played a part. The significance of the story, Richard Shaver's 'I Remember Lemuria', is rather that, in its framework, elements and ideas, it lays out many of the conventions – the ground rules and presuppositions – which are carried forward into the period of flying saucers. These conventions, as we shall see, derive in large part from the theosophical synthesis created by Madame Blavatsky in the 1880s. Other writers (e.g. Partridge 2003; Roth 2005; Kripal 2011; Hammer and Rothstein 2013) have pointed to the links between science fiction's characteristic features and Theosophy; my task is to establish in some detail the justice of this claim, and I have focussed in Blavatsky's work on the role of Spiritualism, on the one hand, and reflection on contemporary scientific advances, on the other.[2] The review of the theosophical imagination presented here offers a worked-out example of improvised thinking with the effects of

1   See Volume I of the series, *Flying Saucers: An Introduction*.
2   I offer further evidence for my claims in the Appendix, where I analyse the key theosophical text in which spirits are projected onto an interplanetary scale for the first time.

scientific advances that is a recurrent topic, a prototype which provides many of the elements, themes and patterns of thought which are repeated in other investigations.

After examining Blavatsky's contribution, I will consider the range of contemporary concerns Shaver's story puts to work within this frame, in this fashion mobilizing the theosophical worldview in the post-war context. In short, we have a discussion of the contribution of Theosophy, framed by Shaver's story. My proposal is that, in a period of technological and scientific innovation driven by warfare and social change, and in a context of recurrent uncertainty as to the traditional bases of both understanding and taking action, Theosophy and its science fiction progeny provided intellectual and moral resources for coping with these conditions, creating a variety of means for making sense of and in this new world condition.

I. The sources of science fiction

Technical developments are of particular concern with regard to the categories of understanding, broadly conceived, because of one common feature: advances in technology undermine certain previously accepted forms of making sense in the world. At the same time as they innovate, they cause a shift in what we may in shorthand call 'definitional space', so that what previously had been problems of measurement become problems of definition. For example, once space flight has become possible, what constitutes a great distance alters, and has altered repeatedly; in addition, questions of the time it takes to travel such distances become a crucial factor. Or, once the atom bomb has been invented, it is no longer clear what defence of the integrity of the self – either of the body or of the nation – might mean (especially once two nations hold the secret), although defence of self and nation was the point of the invention. These two examples present the problem in its clearest form, but every innovation brings its characteristic problems. A series of new technologies created the possibility of recording, storing and transmitting images and sounds without loss of detail and simultaneously posed some unresolvable dilemmas: in short, the concepts of presence and of memory are altered, as is the trust you can place in the representations you are offered. In like fashion, radio allows the immediate presence of a distant voice, so that you can hear thoughts and reports as they happen but in a different place. Here too deception is possible, as in the case of Orson Welles' 1938 broadcast of *The War of the Worlds*, which has taken on a mythical status (see Cantril 2008, originally 1940). Radar, similar in this regard, offers the possibility of detecting things present but invisible to the human eye, and it too can mislead. The invention and development of radio spectroscopy has extended the range where other forms of life might plausibly be found. Every new technology or technical advance not only offers better ways of achieving defined human ends but also has the potential to challenge previously taken for granted assumptions concerning the nature of time and place, human identity and its faculties, and the possibility of other forms of life.

At the same time, then, as the development of the technical possibility of exploring life beyond this planet, there is a parallel history to be traced, a history of speculation about the possibilities and hazards implicated in this exploration and the technological developments which make it feasible. This parallel history can be confined for purposes of starting an investigation to the story of the production of science fiction. Science fiction is a hard-to-define genre, in part because it mixes an intense interest in human manufacture and innovation with many features recalling religious movements, such as apocalyptic fears, aspirations to contact with other minds, utopian hopes, redemptive journeys, election, sacrifices made on the behalf of others, and so on. Furthermore, the sociology of science fiction production is quite complex, involving dynamics of creation, production, edition, and reception, which play reciprocally between authors, publishers, editors and readers. We shall meet both aspects in this investigation.

Attempts at definition of the genre tend to focus on the balance between elements of 'estrangement' (fiction) and 'cognition' (science), or between imagination concerning overcoming the limits of what is possible and the constraints of the real (cf. Suvin 1979). Writers focus on the genre's concern with novelty (again, Suvin on the 'novum') or 'future shock', with human making (Shippey 1992 on 'fabril' literature; cf. Shippey 2016: 26–46), and with future horizons ('archaeologies of the future' in Jameson's term – 2005), together with finding earlier anticipations of these foci in romantic, gothic and symbolist forms (see Aldiss 1983; Seed 1995; Roberts 2000). My concern within this wide field is this: I am interested in the popular fiction in the first part of the twentieth century born of positivism, the literary expression of a commitment to the principle of rational explanation based in a few stable rules. The stories written on that basis were published not only in pulp magazines but also form the classics of the 'Golden Age' of science fiction. And within this corpus, I am interested in how, despite that positivist basis, this fiction exalts in the repeated disturbances of the rule-governed world by scientific and technical innovations. From my perspective, its striking feature is the imaginative space in which science fiction is produced: such writing draws on the power of technological and scientific advances to disturb previously secure ways of making sense. That is its subject matter; it is concerned with changing conditions of thought, an epistemological genre as much as an ethical or speculative one.

Two recent approaches

Two recent works dealing in the history of science fiction provide themes to introduce the path I will take. Both build on Suvin's characterization of the genre. The first is Roberts (2016), who points to the centrality of religious categories in understanding the science fiction imagination and its widespread appeal. His thesis, which he admits is controversial, has a number of strands.

To reduce it to its elements, Roberts suggests, first, that the Protestant Reformation differs from the Catholic settlement in seeking a 'materialist sublime' in the reformed social order, rather than placing trust in the spiritual and magical aspects of the world. Magic is not so much expelled as transformed in its location. Second, this Protestant commitment coincides with and shares in the turn towards a scientific engagement with the natural world, emphasizing observation and experiment. This engagement can be termed 'instrumental' and links Protestantism to early Capitalism and the systematic exploitation of natural resources and the environment. Third, this world-renewing, future-oriented commitment involved a millenarian or utopian strand, seeking a new heaven and a new earth. And fourth, such narratives drew on classical forms, transmitted by Renaissance Humanism, and adopted for their own the ancient form of 'extraordinary voyages', travel not only into strange lands but also into the sky and to other planets, allowing the possibility even of 'time travel'.

In short, we have a this-worldly sublime, engaging with and exploring scientific ideas and technological innovations, expressed in utopian hopes of new lives, new cities, new planets, and taking the fictional form of travel to lands where both these alternative forms to the present and future forms are given expression. For these reasons, Roberts claims that we can find the beginnings of science fiction in this period: 'Science Fiction begins around 1600, as a distinctly Protestant kind of 'fantastic' writing that has budded off from the older (broadly) Catholic traditions of magical and fantastic romances and stories, responding to the new sciences, the advances of which were also tangled up in complex ways with Reformation culture' (Roberts 2016: vi).

More important, he also proposes that this constellation of interests and energies persists and gives a clue to the enduring interest of the genre: 'it is the fierce cultural climate of that time [that] *shaped* SF [science fiction], wrote its DNA in ways that manifest substantively even into the 21st century' (Roberts 2016: vi). Or again, 'my thesis is that the genre as a whole still bears the imprint of the cultural crisis that gave it birth, and that this crisis happened to be a European religious one' (Roberts 2016: 3).

Much of the argument is cast in terms taken from Charles Taylor (1989, 2007), that with the Reformation there was a shift from living worshipfully to living rationally in the world, and that the alliance of Protestantism with scientific rationality, with its emphasis on instrumental thinking and an engagement with technology, can be cast as human life 'moving from a broadly religious understanding of the universe and our place in it ... to a broadly secular one' (Roberts 2016: 20). In short, the Weberian thesis restated: the Reformation gives rise to the modern, secular world. Nevertheless, marks of the Protestant inheritance are to be found in the recurrent science fiction themes of futurism, historicizing the apocalypse, a preoccupation with things going awry and the need for saviour figures (in short, the themes of sin and atonement), as well, Roberts suggests, as a persistent style that combines 'earnest garrulousness and seriousness of approach ... [with] sectarian logic' (Roberts 2016: 507).

On this basis, Roberts builds a detailed history of science fiction; the significant points are the contrast between Verne and Wells (technologies and ideas), the apparent opposition of high-brow (modernist) and low-brow (pulp) science fiction in the first part of the twentieth century, the period of 'hard' science fiction (the 'Golden Age'), the expansion of 'New Wave' (or 'speculative fiction') in the 1960s and 1970s in reaction to the technological sublime of the previous twenty years, and the multiplication of sub-genres in response to both social and technological changes in the more recent period. Roberts' 'systematic' framing of what he regards as the essential core of the science fiction imagination allows both his long retrospective scope and the incorporation of the dialectic between the outside world and the culture of publishing, charting responses to accelerating contextual change and new technologies, including successive new medias of expression, and the related internal dynamics of the industry, in the ever-evolving struggles and re-positioning between fans, on the one hand, and between fans and publishers and critics, on the other.

Roberts' thesis allows him both to read the standard figures and themes of the genre in new ways and to recast that history at certain points, in particular drawing attention to the artificial nature of the distinction between modernist and pulp science fiction literature. The present essay lies within the same broad area, working over a smaller region and looking at the contribution of the liberal Protestant strand to that history.[3]

At the same time, one can have reservations about the broad claim and its expression. In the first place, new research adds to the story and can modify its terms. I would point to Davison's review of the history of

---

[3] I should add, I came to these conclusions by working from another angle than a focus on the history of science fiction, and only read Roberts and other recent histories of science fiction late in the writing process. This essay then offers, to a degree, 'independent confirmation' of his thesis.

Christian doctrine and its 'robustness' with regard to the implications of the discovery of life elsewhere in the universe. It is clear that Catholic theology is something of a straw man in Roberts, and Davison's account could be brought into dialogue with his account of precursors and continuities, specifically concerning the topics of plural worlds and possible multiple incarnations (see Davison 2023). And second, some of Roberts' categories – those of 'science', 'magic', and 'religion' – are too monolithic and demand a more pluralist approach. He appears to be proposing a charter, a core of commitments and rules that seek arbitrarily to constrain the indeterminacy and messiness of social processes.

The second writer I wish to draw on can come in here to supplement Roberts' approach. Vint (2014) covers much the same ground in briefer compass (without the Protestant thesis), but her starting point is to offer what I would call a *genealogy* of the phenomenon rather than a *pedigree*. The terms are not Vint's, but a distinction taken from Geuss (1999), who points out that tracing a pedigree supposes that the value of a project comes from a single origin and descends in a single line of intentional acts aimed at preserving that value, with the added possibility that the longer the line of transmission, the greater the value. A genealogy, in contrast, does not seek to legitimize a present practice and does not seek to identify a single origin. Instead, it identifies 'the historically contingent conjunction of … separate processes that ramify the further back one goes and present no obvious or natural single stopping place that could be designated "the origin"' (Geuss 1999: 4). Rather than a transmission of consciously held values, we are dealing in contingencies and points of change, forking paths, indeed, with different and incompatible outcomes in the present.

Working along these lines, Vint moves away from any single definition of the genre, existing in principle outside history, of which one then finds examples, prompting debate whether instances should be included or excluded from the category. So, while she expends a certain effort on defining characteristic 'myths' and 'icons', she points out we need to think instead of 'the cultural work performed by such icons' and the function of the mythologies created, which 'help us grasp the experience of human life in a world dominated by scientific thinking' (Vint 2014: 5). The characteristic myths may well be what other critics term 'sub-genres'; Vint defines these as 'providing imaginary solutions to the real contradictions and tensions of a world in which science has replaced religion as the hegemonic explanatory discourse, a world in which the products of technoscience are ubiquitous in everyday life' (Vint 2014: 4).[4] And Vint proposes that 'icons' 'perform this kind of cultural work when they become detached [from their fictional setting and gain] … currency in the popular culture at large' (Vint 2014: 4–5; she is quoting Wolfe 2011). These icons are motifs such as 'alien encounters, robots and other created beings, travel through time or outer space, apocalyptic or perfected futures, posthuman descendants and Artificial Intelligences' (Vint 2014: 5), though the list can be neither definitive nor closed.

These myths and icons mark a work as science fictional but, as Vint makes clear, listing them does not explain how they work nor which ones might be employed in any given story. She therefore looks at cases which we might think of as points of precipitation – Gernsback's 1926 manifesto, for example – and reflects on the sources being brought together and the redefinition of the past this implies, as well as reviewing the interests present – commercial, literary, political and other – in the context of production. She then considers developments as these claims are put to work in new contexts, by new parties, and the debates that result from these redeployments. In short, she offers a genealogy, looking at the assemblage of contingent actors, forces, clusters of interests, models and circumstances that meet one another, shaping and influencing stories that then can go on to be put to work for new ends elsewhere. These moments of encounter provide the subject matter for the several chapters of her book, reviewing the major theories and topics that have shaped the scholarship of the subject and allowing a sketch of that series of events which is the best one can do to provide a history of the genre. No essence, then, and no founding moment; simply a series of events and responses, when materials are taken up and put to new purposes, with no overarching end or purpose.

A consistent theme in such an account is the relation between realism and imagination, or science and fiction (or cognition and estrangement).

---

4   We might think once again that 'science' and 'religion' are too monolithic as categories to serve well in the pluralistic world she is seeking to describe.

We have a world dominated by science and technology and the imaginative response to this situation, both a celebration and a sense of anxiety, is a series of imaginary solutions signalled by a series of icons. And, if we follow the genealogical argument, it is not a single world, construed from a single viewpoint, 'science' (and formerly by 'religion'), but there are distinct sciences, each with their own history, demanding separate responses; a world then which cannot be experienced as such, grasped from a single viewpoint, but one oriented around successive and not necessarily coherent 'problems', caused in the main by the breakdown of previously secure categories for making sense and, furthermore, disturbed or provoked by the promise of successive 'solutions'. 'Cognitive estrangement' might in this light be seen as an action-oriented mindset confronted by repeated moments which cannot be either grasped or resolved by this mindset: a recurring experience of the failure of decisive action and technological resources to resolve problems. Instead, the interventionist approach generates problems at various scales (illusion, addiction, chances for exploitation, deception, material disadvantage, disaster, even apocalypse). All these questions – summed up as Is it nature? Is it us? – are resolved into a plurality of worlds (or a fragmented world condition), experienced as an oscillation between realist initiatives and imaginative readings.

In short, what we take from these two contemporary accounts is, on the one hand, a continuing place for religious categories and investments and, on the other, a genealogical approach rather than seeking a pedigree or any single origin.

II. The 'Shaver Mystery'

I want to examine a particular story in this perspective, Richard Shaver's 'I Remember Lemuria', published in *Amazing Stories* in 1945. This example has been widely discussed; the case has been made that this story – and others by its author, collectively known as the 'Shaver Mystery' – played a key role in precipitating the era of flying saucer sightings which began in

1947 with a report by Kenneth Arnold. The stories have come to be seen as having prepared the ground for sightings, providing some important categories for their apprehension and reception, and so participating dialectically in their production and reporting. The question is, what precisely did the stories contribute? To anticipate the answer, Shaver's achievement was not to have invented flying saucers, but to have prepared the space for them by bringing together a paranoid vision – things are not what they seem in our society – with Theosophy's understanding of a populated universe operating over a vast time scale.

I draw attention to three issues concerning this choice of story, to be explored to different degrees. In the first place, Shaver has not always been included as part of the history of flying saucer sightings; the identification of his role itself has a recent history. Second, his work is not high art within the science fiction genre, but rather, although constructed using recognizable tropes, comes from well towards the 'pulp' end of the spectrum. This fact is significant if one is considering where the lasting influence of popular forms such as science fiction may be produced: it emerges less in individual acts of writing than in collective discussions created through the activity not only of writers but also of readers, who respond through letters and testimonies. The idea of flying saucers is in good part produced through shared 'workshops' found in pulp magazines and fanzines; the movement 'writes itself into existence' in this shared milieu, paralleling a great many other movements including mesmerism and spiritualism in the United States a hundred years earlier. And third, although Shaver's influence has been well argued for, I am not sure the particular significance of his writing has been properly identified, and so the contribution he made, which his audience drew on and helped to elaborate, fully appreciated.

First, Shaver's role, and that of his editor and effective co-author, Ray Palmer, have not always been part of the narrative. They are absent, for example, from Jacobs' standard history, *The UFO Controversy in America*, published in 1975. They owe their prominence to an article, 'The Man Who Invented Flying Saucers', by John Keel, published in 1986. They then appear as an established part of the story in, for instance, Peebles (1994) and Kripal (2011). Keel was a journalist who investigated flying saucer reports and who offers a perceptive, shrewd and informed account of that history, one that takes seriously the ordinary people who constitute the bulk of the witnesses. Keel's focus is on Palmer's role (Keel 2014: 117): he argues that Palmer anticipated the idea of the flying saucer, that he caused the topic to be taken seriously, rather than simply being fodder for 'silly season' journalism, and that he kept the subject alive during periods of public disinterest and few reports (identified as the years between 1957 and 1964 and then 1969 to 1973). We are concerned particularly with his role during the initial period around the end of the War.

Keel places Palmer (1911–1977) in a particular milieu; Palmer was a reader of pulp magazines and an active participant in the 'subculture of mimeographed "fanzines" and abundant interpersonal correspondence' in the 1920s, then a writer of science fiction stories from 1930 and, from 1938, editor of *Amazing Stories*, a pulp created by Hugo Gernsback in 1926 but with a declining readership a decade later.[5] Keel was also an active youthful participant in the same milieu in the 1940s, and he rated *Amazing Stories* as 'the very worst' of the dozen or so science fiction magazines sold on the newsstands, with poor editing, sensational and outdated storylines, and a series of unskilled writers, often drawn from the fan scene. The magazine owed its success to a single story, 'I Remember Lemuria', by Richard Shaver, published in 1945, and to its sequels.

The history of the writing of 'I Remember Lemuria' is given by Kripal (2011: 99–103; cf. Palmer 1975: 136ff.). Shaver wrote a letter in September 1943 to Palmer, which Palmer published in the first issue of 1944. The letter offered a 'little treatise on an alleged twenty-six-lettered "ancient alphabet", which … Shaver believed … was "definite proof of the Atlantean legend"' (Kripal 2011: 99).[6] Palmer also wrote back to Shaver asking about

5   Palmer's history and the milieu of pulp publishing and audiences is traced in detail by Toronto (2013), who draws on Moskowitz (1974) and Warner (1970) as well as a good deal of original research. Other sources include Palmer (1975) and Wentworth (1973). For a recent account of Shaver and Palmer, see Halperin (2020), chapter 7. For a discussion of the particular features of science fiction fan culture, see Vint (2014), chapter 6.

6   The alphabet was later called 'Mantong' [= Man's Tongue], and is, according to Kripal, 'nothing more than the English alphabet related to a series of … literalistic puns and free associations … which are then used to imagine a series of false

the source of the alphabet, and Shaver replied with a 10,000 word typed story entitled 'A Warning to Future Man', setting out 'an elaborate, deeply paranoid cosmology that Shaver claimed had been revealed to him by voices he heard emanating from the ground'. Palmer took Shaver's story and turned it into a 31,000-word piece, published in *Amazing Stories* in March 1945 (Kripal 2011: 101).

This co-authored story evoked a remarkable response from its readers; sales doubled (Keel 2014: 120), and thousands of letters were received, claiming the readers recognized the kind of experiences recorded and had shared them. In essence, these experiences supported a vision of a world ordered by strange beings unsympathetic to human concerns, who plagued human lives and controlled thoughts; the letters also offered supporting 'evidence', describing strange objects seen in the skies and strange encounters with alien beings.

Shaver had written a series of loosely related stories which Palmer purchased and published subsequently; Palmer indeed devoted himself to promoting the 'Shaver Mystery', apparently from a mixture of commitment and commercial acumen. Wentworth (1973) suggests that Palmer's persistence arose from his sharing what we might call Shaver's vision, expressed both in his giving up his editorship of the journal, in the face of opposition to a continued focus on Shaver's stories, and in his moving to live near the writer. Toronto (2013) offers a more nuanced account. Nevertheless, the key appears to be Shaver's vision or worldview, into which the business of flying saucers could be fitted when they emerged in 1947. It was Shaver's worldview that stimulated a wide readership as well as inspiring Palmer and is the eventual concern of this reading.

Palmer gave up the editorship of *Amazing Stories* in 1949, left Chicago, moving to live close to the Shaver household in Wisconsin, and went fully independent, setting up his own publishing house and press just as

---

etymologies' (Kripal 2011: 100), a device employed in filling out the stories. It may well be taken over from the 'Adam-Man Tongue' invented in 1903 by Webster Cleverly (1852–1926), who published a series of books under the name Edmund Shaftesbury on animal magnetism (mesmerism).

the market for pulp magazines collapsed.[7] Palmer launched, edited and published a series of low-circulation magazines over the next twenty-five years: the series began with a new journal, *FATE* (launched in 1948), which carried reports of flying saucers in every issue; it carried on with *Other Worlds* (1950), then *Mystic* (1954), retitled as *Search* in 1956, which printed readers' letters and articles on the occult, followed by *Flying Saucers from Other Worlds* (1957), later shortened to *Flying Saucers*, and other titles such as *Universe* and *Space World*. By 1966, he had dropped *FATE*, *Other Worlds* and *Universe*, though *Search*, *Flying Saucers* and *Space World* continued in print, and that year started two new publications, *Forum*, a discussion group consisting of editorial comment and readers' responses, organized around such topics as conspiracy theories, reincarnation and angels, and a sixteen-volume reprint of the Shaver Mystery materials called *Hidden World*. *Flying Saucers* closed in 1975, and *Search* ceased publication on Palmer's death in 1977 (see Toronto 2013: 226f.; Keel 2014: 121–125). In Keel's view, Palmer organized the informal milieu in which discussion of flying saucers took place over three decades; he kept the subject on the agenda during dry periods, and he set the terms in which flying saucers were viewed: essentially, mechanisms directed by intentional life forms, presumed by most interested parties to be of interplanetary origin.

Shaver's story then emerged in a recognizable world: an autodidact milieu, with a commitment to a scientific worldview taken to focus on experience as fact, and a belief in the power of 'democratic education': that people could learn the truth about the contemporary world and share it, against the conspiracies to conceal on the part of established interests. The bottom end of the pulp market bears a strong resemblance in these regards to the earlier world of 'plebeian' spiritualism (see Barrow 1986); it presents

---

7   Keel suggests that the market for pulps was undermined by post-War inflation and the advent of television; we might wonder, too, about the campaign in the name of public morality against pulp magazines and comics in particular – see Fredric Wertham's *The Seduction of the Innocent* (1954), cf. Beaty (2005). There was also a subtle shift in the literature's concerns and focus, from machines to minds, in the same period, which may have contributed.

a worldview that contains a theodicy, an account of the possibilities of human flourishing and an explanation of human woes.

Keel is therefore beside the point when he suggests that the appeal of Shaver's writings was principally to readers who shared forms of paranoid-schizophrenia, often expressed in political philosophies reflecting 'their own fears and insecurities' (Keel 2014: 120). He also links this psychological tendency to the desire to find evidence of 'some distinctly non-terrestrial group in our midst', in the extra-terrestrial hypothesis. My suggestion is that Shaver's work is significant on a wider social scale and cannot be reduced to an individual-focussed psychological reading (which is a common tendency among those authors who cite him, and for which Shaver's biography on the surface offers a good deal of supporting evidence – see Toronto 2013).

If Shaver's story played a significant role in the precipitation of the flying saucer events in 1947, as is claimed repeatedly, it was neither by reproducing individual paranoid symptoms nor was it by anticipation of the phenomena: the story (as we shall see) was a conventional 'space opera'[8] of the period, a melodramatic, interplanetary adventure, and contained no predictive elements of technologies or sightings. Its contribution lay, rather, in offering a persuasive theodicy in the context.

III. Shaver's story

Let us turn to the story. 'I Remember Lemuria' contains an account of the text's origin while at the same time offering an interpretation of the reader's world. A message from the past, it draws attention to certain hitherto unremarked features of this present world – to certain anomalies – and proposes an explanation of these. A parallel is drawn between the past condition and the present, and the reader is challenged either to accept or reject the explanation offered of anomalous features common to both.

---

8   The term is a parallel to radio 'soap operas' and was first used in the early 1940s.

The story is constructed around two distinct elements: first, a clear account of certain crucial features of the world and its potential, construed in scientific terms that derive from a specific background and tradition, and second, a dawning mistrust concerning surface appearances. The first appears notably in a focus on the possibilities of direct mental communication and a pervasive vitalism, the second in a sense of needing to get behind appearances in order to gain insight into the truth of the situation.

I will outline the plot before considering the various themes that appear in it; we shall then turn (in the following chapter) to the role of Theosophy in creating the ground rules of the story, before finally returning to the story to offer a reading in terms of the employment of these ground rules in a narrative of distrust and analysing the theodicy it offers. We might put Shaver's achievement as follows: a largely theosophical worldview is mobilized to describe crucial features of the War period, characterized by the combination of effects produced by new military technologies and new forms of media.

The plot

The protagonist and narrator, Mutan Mion, living in the subterranean city of Sub-Atlan, is sent to study science in the capital, Tean City, located at the centre of the planet Mu (an abbreviation of Lemuria). The narrative is marked by an enthusiasm for technical detail, containing a number of invented abbreviations, colloquialisms and technical terms, and both the constructed vocabulary and rather high-flown style of narration add to the atmosphere of the story. I quote extensively from the text because the style and energy with which the story is told mark the object we are seeking to understand.[9]

Despite appearances of enormous vitality, life in Tean City is troubled beneath the surface; we are given hints of fears and of hidden forces at work, and then witness an outbreak of violence. Mutan with the help of fellow

---

9   I give no page references because there is no standard edition from which to cite. I used a reprint, Shaver (2016).

students begins to piece together aspects of this hidden situation and its causes, aided by one of their teachers who, however, then disappears. The group, alarmed by this, therefore decide to escape from the planet which, despite widespread practices of thought monitoring by the authorities, they succeed in doing. They gain the surface of the planet and hire a spaceship – ostensibly for a leisure flight – outrun their pursuers by a trick and reach the planet Quanto.

There they report on the true state of affairs on Mu (as far as they understand it) to the planet's rulers, the Nortans, and attach themselves to the court of the Princess Vanue. The Nortans form a fleet with the intention of invading Mu and rescuing its citizens from the hidden forces that have come to undermine their security and well-being. The Princess is the leader of this force and the defecting Atlans, as they are called, return with her.

The last third of the story consists of the campaign on Mu, the gradual revelation of the powers hidden in subterranean tunnels, and their defeat. At the same time, the victory over evil cannot be total: the physical causes that explain the degeneration of vitality suffered cannot be eliminated, so the population of the planet must be deported to other places. Mutan is given the task of creating a record explaining the history and its meaning, to be left for future generations of those who remain on the planet by accident or their own design. In this fashion, it becomes clear, first, that Mu (Lemuria) is Earth at an earlier stage and, so, how the story comes into the reader's hands and, last, why it explains certain features of the present human condition: in terms of Shaver's original title, it is 'A Warning to Future Man'.

The plot has a familiar shape. The world of appearances is gradually undermined by glimpses of more sinister elements, leading to the protagonist's flight both because he has begun to decipher the secret and because hidden actors suspect his intentions. He assembles an alliance and returns to right the situation, and in this process of returning things to a proper order both reveals the ground rules that explain the plot and creates the record which can travel through time and reach its intended reader, making clear those same ground rules may operate in the present.

A number of striking themes emerge in the course of the narrative: a subterranean world, vitalism embodied in both higher and lower races, degeneration expressed both in natural and social-historical forms, and a secret history of the world linking these features (cf. Kripal 2011). It is worth laying these out, before looking at their sources and style of employment.

A subterranean world

The first is the motif of a subterranean world, a world hidden from view, with many levels. We first meet Mutan in Sub-Atlan, a city just beneath the surface of the planet Mu, communicating with the outside. The surface is known as Atlan or Atlantis, and is largely natural, although it has certain built features. But the cities lie beneath the surface, the largest, Tean City, lying at the centre of the planet. The different levels are joined by elevators, so one may pass from nature on the outside to the sophisticated scientific culture at the centre. The system of caves and cities is of great antiquity, some of which have been abandoned, along with their complexes of tunnels. These underground complexes were made in the early, energetic days of the planet's life.

The subterranean world is subject to conflicting evaluations. In his narration, Mutan indicates no discomfort with this underground existence, and only enthusiasm for the subterranean cities, especially the wonders of Tean City. At the same time, he has no fear of the surface, nor of interplanetary flight. And yet conspiracies and secrets can mature underground, hidden from sight in the abandoned caves and tunnels; danger comes from within.

The notion of underground worlds is not of course original to Shaver. Kripal (2011: 32–36)[10] traces earlier instances of the hollow world thesis. From our point of view, the most significant example in this tradition is Edward Bulwer-Lytton's *The Coming Race* (1871), which sets the discovery of a new civilization under the earth's surface. It is significant because of its articulation of the idea of the 'coming race': we meet with life forms representing our future, or our replacements. The coming race is a recurrent idea in the late nineteenth century, not least in the notion of spirits, who

---

10 Drawing on Standish (2006).

may be more evolved forms travelling back in time to try to assist us and speed up our progress as a race.

Vitalism

Bulwer-Lytton's account also introduces a form of vitalism, which is the second theme I wish to identify in Shaver's story. In *The Coming Race*, the new civilization is built around (to quote Kripal 2011: 44) 'a mysterious electromagnetic-spiritual energy called *vril* … employed … to both mystical and technological ends'. Vril is likened not only to 'electricity or magnetism' but also to the 'mysterious forces at work in "mesmeric clairvoyance"': it is used to 'cut rocks and build cities, power vehicles, control "automaton figures" … light lamps, [and] direct engineering projects'; it also can 'render [the body] super conductive to its own natural healing energies … induce various altered states of consciousness, like trance and vision, through which thoughts can be transferred from one brain to another'. Vril also carries 'patently erotic overtones, particularly in the females'. Shaver's vitalism shares all these features. It appears in the variety of actors portrayed, who are distinguished precisely by their different levels of vital energy (expressed in size, knowledge, wisdom, and virility), and then in the positive role of energy in the organization and working of the society of the Atlans (and of the Nortans).

The Atlans are a hierarchical society, ordered by vitality expressed in many respects. The ruling figures – the Titans – are of great size, long lived, immensely attractive (especially the females), wise and with extraordinary mental powers and energy. Mutan is of the lesser orders; he is a 'culture man, a product of the laboratories';[11] we see the incubators in which human embryos are grown in the medical school laboratories in Tean City. The role of technicians is central, for the processes of growth are protected by 'technicons', who control every aspect of their development. We are given other hints of the technicons' constructive power in the extraordinary

---

11   Culture men also refer to themselves as the 'mediocro', without apparent irony or resentment.

variety of hybrid body forms of the citizens, as well as the hybrids' beauty, vitality and intelligence. Technicons are drawn from the Titan race. These experts construct not only biological form but every aspect of social life, including the formation of the culture people. During his early formation, Mutan roamed in the 'culture forests of Atlan' on the surface of the planet, while, in his later education, the class are regularly given drugs to make them more receptive and to stimulate new ideas. Life is highly constructed and programmed. As we shall see, there is a flaw in this overreliance on technical expertise to promote social life and the vitality of the citizens, even when guided by superior intelligence.

This emphasis on a technically controlled, vital environment is reflected in the architecture and public art of Tean City. Moreover, this technical enhancement of life goes far beyond the educational function of public architecture and decoration; we learn, for instance, about the detailed production of intensified sensation in the dance which Mutan and his variform fellow student Arl attend: beyond the paintings which 'show the way to participation in love and joy', the dancers' nerves are stimulated by electromagnetic frequencies of 'appropriate attunements', and the stimulating rays made them intensely aware of the 'electric pressure of the (other's) body aura'; moreover, the 'odor music of the Atlans wove into the sound music many scent accompaniments ... feeding the nerves'.

There is a generalized word for this all-purpose energy which can be controlled and experienced: 'exd' (which must correspond to Bulwer-Lytton's 'vril'). We are introduced to this idea when Mutan's Titan teacher explains the source of energy to the class. He speaks of the cyclical lives of suns and planets: a planet circles around a sun, developing a covering of forests and depositing coal; the sun ages and dies, and the planet dies too, remaining as a store of potential heat with its thick shell of carbon; a meteor from another sun strikes the dead planet and ignites the carbon, creating a new sun; the new sun emits heat and light, creating life on a daughter planet's surface, and so on. The instructor continues: 'the carbon fire ... [is] a clean fire ... the atoms of carbon, when disintegrated, send forth the beneficial energy ash called exd which can be assimilated by our bodies and used to promote life-growth'. This is a myth dealing in radiation – resulting from the disintegration of atoms – and the emission of rays which can be harnessed for positive ends but which also, as we shall learn, can produce negative effects. Exd recurs through the first part of the story.

Technical mastery at this sub-atomic level underlies the controlled world of intensified sensation which strikes the newly arrived Mutan repeatedly, in the architecture and the dance, and in the manufactured multiple forms and the bodily appeal of the creatures he encounters. In such a constructed and controlled environment, everything depends on the technicians, teachers and leaders, the Titans. These are of a different race to the products of the culture laboratories, although they exert a benign power of a most intimate sort over these constructed creatures.

The size of the Titans relates to their great vitality; the same principles apply among the Nortans: Princess Vanue was a 'huge figure which was an immense concentration of all the vitally stimulating qualities that make beauty the sought-for thing that it is'. There is also a political class of Titan ruling elders among the Atlans, responsible for the direction of the society and making all important decisions as well as for its administration and communication with the populace. We learn less about this ruling elite, although this is where the hidden weaknesses of the society manifest themselves.

At first sight, then, Mu is a technologically advanced society containing great inequalities of power and knowledge between races, inequalities which are compensated for by both by the benignity of the elites and the appearance of their natural superiority, their fitness to rule. The culture men and women are stimulated, taught and entertained; they are politically irresponsible consumers. This is the portrayal of a modern society dominated by information and technologies of communication – rays and the like – where political and other decision making does not concern the bulk of the population, whose task is to consume and to obey instructions.

The problems arise when the appearances of this benign society break down, when the charisma of the leaders falters, and further races appear, this time degenerate products of detrimental energies. Hidden forces – secrets – appear. What do we know about these degenerate forms?

Sources of degeneration

Whilst we have been instructed about the natural vitality of the older races, together with the artificially enhanced lives of the hybrid culture men and women, and about the expression of this vitality simultaneously in stature, wisdom, age and power of sexual attraction, at the same time we learn about the possibility of the loss of this vitality and degeneration. Indeed, the processes of degeneration drive the narrative. These processes of degeneration have two aspects, to do with the effects of the ageing sun's rays and the origins of sickness and death, on the one hand, and with the hidden conspiracies that result from these effects, on the other. Vitalism has its dark side.

As we have seen, the Titan teacher instructs the class on the cycle whereby planets turn into suns and feed life on further planets. But he adds a crucial detail: 'a carbon fire is a clean fire and contains no dense metals like radium, titanium, uranium, polonium – whose emanations in disintegrance in suns cause old age and death because minute particles given off accumulate and convey the ever-fire into the body, there to kill it in time'. Young suns do not emit these noxious forms of radiation from the heavy metals, and on a planet under such a sun there is no ageing, and the only form of death is by accident, during the period of youthful education on the surface, for example. As we have learned, the disintegrated carbon atoms emit 'beneficial energy ash called exd', promoting life-growth.

However, the heavy metals lie at the core of the sun and are consumed after the shell of carbon has been partly burned away, and 'when these heavy elements begin to disintegrate in the ever-fire … we come to the cause of age'. The Titan continues: 'The particles of radium and other radioactive metals are the poison that causes the aging of tissue'. This is the condition which pertains potentially on Mu. He explains that Mu's sun throws out 'great masses of these poisonous particles. They fall upon Mu in a continual flood, entering into living tissue and infecting it with the radioactive disease we call age'. The poisons accumulate in the soil and contaminate the water, and so are absorbed into the body, halting growth and – worse – preventing 'any effectual use of exd, which is the food of all integration'.

There is a major technical effort to resist this threat to vitality. The technicons devise means of protection from the 'accumulations of the age poisons' by such means as distillation and centrifugation of water and the creation of magnetic fields of 'ben [benign?] energies'. Yet these methods are not perfect, and the population is losing energy, maturity and length of life; finally, the Titan concludes, 'death will strike us all'. Detrimental energies have their parallels in New Thought, Christian Science and Scientology (the latter contemporary to Shaver).

This is a striking reflection on the physical implications of the discovery of radiation.[12] In Shaver's story, the solution lies initially in the hands of experts. The first step may have been to retreat below the surface of the planet to subterranean cities and systems of tunnels, although their antiquity argues that these constructions may come from an earlier phase of the sun's history. But the technicons' present plan is to remove the population to another planet. 'I learned that the coordinators and rodite [another term for the caste of technicians] were preparing the plans and ships for our migration to a young, new-born sun, where the force setup of life conditions left a greater margin of exd for intake of power, where integrance went on at a faster pace, and [a hint of things to be explained] where the infection that caused the occasional trouble with detrimental energy robotism or detrimental err in the human did not occur'.

It is worth remarking that the guarantee of the sanity of the leaders of the planet Quanto, to which the group of Atlan students make their escape, is that it is a sunless planet and so without the threat of radiation.

---

12   There are parallels with a contemporary science fiction story by Robert Heinlein. In 'Waldo' (1940), new forms of energy and communication – atomic power and radio waves – are amalgamated in the concept of radiation. And radiation alters the ground rules of reality, not only causing hidden debilitation in humans but also creating new possibilities in the world, allowing thought to have direct effects. Radiation, indeed, reveals the idealist nature of reality; previously, the laws of Physics have only held because of people's unthinking adherence to them; as their minds weaken under the influence of these invisible rays, physical laws multiply and mind's power over matter is made clear. Heinlein's approach is a good deal more optimistic than Shaver's, and Waldo's genius first discerns and then resolves the problem of mind over matter.

There, vitality develops unimpeded: as evidence, size is not only proportional to the age of the individual, but also to the age of the parent when the individual is conceived. As a consequence, the Nortans show, even in comparison to Mu, extraordinary technical, scientific and mental advancement, which enables them, among other skills, to read their visitors' thoughts and to evaluate the threat they announce. They also are able to communicate telepathically. Their society is an extreme expression of the tendencies we have encountered: their elder, Princess Vanue, exceeds the vitality and attraction of Mu's Titans, so that Mutan's love and loyalty is drawn to her in 'ecstatic desire'; in a similar fashion, in the ensuing interplanetary conflict, the loyalty of defecting Atlan ships is assured simply by placing on each a Nortan female elder to whom the male warriors become devoted. It is a society organized around the erotic desire of women (a theme often expressed in the covers of pulp magazines, though rarely more than hinted at in the texts).

In short, Shaver's Lemuria is a world of well-organized appearances, on the surface a peaceable society, run by benign experts and organized around the worship of women's erotic power, appearances which are however threatened by invisible radiation, the product of radioactive elements emitted by the sun as it ages.

The second aspect of degeneration concerns the social and political consequences of this invisible radiation, consequences which involve not only the corruption of minds but also the creation of a new race, as we shall see. These forms of degeneracy first emerge in the secret fears Mutan detects beneath the confident appearances of Tean City.

For the fears detected by Mutan do not relate simply to these 'age poisons'. The Titan teacher talks about a deeper fear, having first sought to protect their discussion from outside listeners. He speaks of a need for secrecy because of constant screening by 'spying rays' which detect suspicion or knowledge in minds; the result of detection by these rays is death before any possibility of counteraction. He then speaks of clues, rumours, and the deciphering of a mystery. He has heard that 'certain groups of Atlans are against the projected migration, and the recent disappearance of several men important to our work lends color to the story'. He reasons that the only possible source of such a conspiracy (though he does not use the word) could be a group of key technicons (rodite) at the centre of things, that for unknown reasons they have become corrupted and, worse, that this condition goes unchecked. And he makes a hypothesis, linking the state of affairs to the bad effects of radiation: that 'some of these [rodite] may have accidentally suffered a severe flashback of detrimental ion flow, so that their will has become one under detrimental hypnosis'.

The teacher makes clear to the young class that their task is to 'seek out the information that will clear the way for the migration'. They have to join in this process of reading signs and deciphering the processes behind appearances.

They are more or less immediately confronted with their task. Some of them go to the dance with its 'enhanced delights' produced by technicians, and a son of a Titan is struck down by a death ray, which is then turned on other dancers; there is no security present. Mutan realizes one aspect of reality: 'It is true; our perfect government is not so perfect after all'.

Mutan and Arl attach themselves to a group leaving the chaos, seeking to escape the attention of the hostile mind observing the consequences of his action. They overhear discussion of a rumour to the effect that the migration is cover for the elite to escape to a new sun, leaving behind them the remnant of the population lacking the resources to follow and share the new world. Such a selfish programme, the speaker continues, could only be the product of 'detrimental energy', for it contains a contradiction: the elite, to be in a condition to refuse 'all ... normal units of life's fabric the right to existence and growth', would have to have become 'dull and lifeless robots ... besotted with detrimental energy' and therefore incapable of building any social fabric to replace what they had destroyed.

We should note that robotism here is a condition living things – humans – can fall into, not a name for machines, even if it is a machine-like condition. It is a parasitic attitude: the self-interested group denies the mutual dependency of social life upon which it draws; in short, it exploits its short-term advantages with little thought for the long-term. How is such a contradictory attitude possible, the speaker asks, in a seemingly well-ordered world?

Mutan takes up the discussion, drawing on his recent instruction: in a condition of 'detrimental hypnosis', the mind 'confuses its self-originated impulses with the exterior-originated detrimental impulses to destroy. Such a condition is called dero, or detrimental energy robotism'. As his thinking develops, he supposes that the migration may have been delayed too long, that the old sun's 'disintegrant pressure' has caused too profound an error in the 'control of minds about us', and that the breaking of secrecy by the open use of the death ray at the dance indicates 'the plan of the rodite must be near completion'.

Beneath appearances, then, a point of crisis is approaching. The next day, the class discovers their teacher is absent, supposed ill – an almost unheard-of condition. They fear his instruction had been overheard by the evil rodite, despite the precaution of a guard ray, and that their lives too are threatened. Although they can articulate nothing, for even thoughts can be read by unseen listeners, together they plan a visit to the surface of the planet and then their escape from Mu.

I have two connected comments to make. The first concerns the spectrum of radiation at work. It first appears as a source of energy, vitality and growth – exd – from the sun, and then as detrimental energy from the burning of heavy metals, causing ageing, disease and death. But these forms of energy can be mobilized and put to work by technicians, controlled to produce forms of teaching, healing and growth, as well as pleasure, or perverted into death rays. These rays are put to work to protect ('ben' energy) and guard, and to listen, to overhear unseen, to monitor the population. They also relate to the business of private communications within the elite and, as we shall see, to public broadcasts informing the population. And they link to the ability to read thoughts, both with and without the consent of the person whose mind is read.

All these powers are ambiguous only in the sense that the narrator, Mutan, judges the uses to which they are put or, more precisely, the side on which they operate. He has no qualms, for example, about the forcing of the minds of captured enemy to gain vital intelligence. He lives in a world of brain waves, radio waves and radiation, and these forms convey information, which is ethically neutral.

The second comment concerns the need to decipher the ends to which this information is put. The narrator begins in a world of appearances, on the surface a benign world. He then gains clues and hears rumours which neither conform to the surface nor add up readily to another account. He has to seek out the truth behind appearances, by questioning, following clues, overhearing others, going back over earlier material and questioning his previous understanding. Understanding is only created through research. He begins to understand that his picture of the world has been constructed, by technicians in the laboratories, in his education, through the public media; he also learns that perceptions are created by drugs and invisible forms made by hidden groups of experts. It is a Brave New World. The world he discovers is one of signs, but signs created by technical media, whose rationale remains concealed. And he begins to piece together evidence of a conspiracy, of a group of technicians not governed by the common interest (a theme Huxley avoids in 1932).

This approach is not unlike film noir, which flourished contemporary to Shaver's writing; much has been made of Shaver's periods of mental illness, but he portrays a recognizable contemporary world, one where an anomalous event can only be understood through a series of flashbacks and reconstructions, where groups of people try to manipulate the narratives that are disseminated and to conceal their interests from other third parties (and where women control men's desires to their own purposes). This is a paranoid world, but the paranoia is a social, not an individual, mental, condition.

Somewhat like film noir, Shaver's story does not peter out in a world constructed of manipulations of narratives or exchanges of information without any underlying rationale (a vision which is tried out, for example, in some of Dashiell Hammett's work). Instead, he works to reveal a second narrative behind the first, one in which detrimental energy has triumphed. Conspiracy theory is necessary for a narrative to emerge.

A secret history

The extent of the corruption of the elite, or the replacement of the elite by corrupt elements, only emerges in the course of the Nortan invasion with the aim of restoring the status quo. The story here develops in stages.

The approaching fleet is detected, and a threat uttered: the Atlan population are effectively hostages and will be killed in the event of any attempted invasion to liberate them. There is therefore a need for complete secrecy, and the Nortan plan exploits the same conditions as the corrupt elements have manipulated in the past: the total reliance of the society on technologies of communication, and the extreme centralization of power that accompanies this system of government.

The Nortan fleet retreats into space, leaving behind a single ship under Vanue's command, hidden in the moon's shadow, with some accompanying Atlan allies, their loyalty commanded by their desire. Mutan is returned home to Mu by one of these men in a small craft, as an undercover agent. The ship then causes the population of Sub Atlan to fall asleep by means of rays, and Mutan and four comrades, protected from the rays by a device they carry, enter the administration building with the objective of turning off the warning systems and corralling any opposition capable of coordinating a defence and then guiding in the invading craft.

The administration centre works through telecommunications: it is called the 'telemechro center'. We are told that the telenews for citizens speaks of nothing significant; it does not, for example, mention the near invasion. In the centre, however, there are numerous screens allowing the continual monitoring of the entire city, and the communication system allows both coordination between technicians and control of the citizens. Surveillance, communication and active control are all achieved by the transmission of rays or beams.

In the building we encounter the somewhat startling operators of this system, a distinct race, the 'abandondero', dwarfs from the abandoned caverns, 'clothed in rags and dirt ... their hair long and matted'. One of the Atlan comrades explains their origins: 'When the machinery became defective from age, many centuries ago, a vast number of caverns were sealed up. Fugitives hid in them, used the defective pleasure stimulators, and as a result, their children were these things./They die of age, are stupid, cannot even read or write'.

These products of pleasure-stimulating machines gone wrong (rather than simply the wrong kind of radiation) however are incapable of self-organization. The informant adds: 'they must have a vicious, cunning leader who has learned to use them'. Mutan sums up what we have learned so far: 'these ugly dwarfs ... were dero, children of dero, enslaved in some manner by the derodite master who sought the death of all Mu!'. If 'dero' stands for detrimental energy robot (which, I repeat, does not here imply a machine), then 'derodite' signifies detrimental energy rodite or technician.

In the next phase of the operation, the captured deros are placed under the mental control of Nortan maids, themselves expressions of the 'augmented will' of Princess Vanue, and the sleep ray switched off, so that the appearance of normal life is restored, but the communication centre under new management, as secret as the previous regime. Communication is re-established with Tean City, and behind the speaker there we glimpse in the monitor a further insight into the corrupt regime: there are some Atlan elders being tortured and 'drunken renegades from Atlan's army ... dragging protesting girls after them', in celebration of the supposed frustration of the Nortan fleet.

Having exploited the communication system to deceive – repeating the trick of the derodite elite – the Nortan invasion can continue in secret, bringing in troops and setting up control apparatuses. Everything depends upon the control of appearances and the construction of a different – military – reality behind the controlled images of normality.

At the same time, the secrets of the abandondero are extracted by mind reading, and the location of the conspiracy discovered to be outside the cities, in the 'abandoned caverns ... [and the] sealed cities'. Two of the captured creatures are taken to the mother ship and submitted to further detailed examination in a 'telaug' [telepathic augmenter?] and, in the course of gaining practical information, the recent secret history of the planet emerges.

This history connects government by information, the rise of the technocrats, and the inevitable centralization of power under these conditions. The growing dominance of the derodite had been concealed precisely because of the 'centralizing of all power by the rodite method of government'; once the 'central rodite synchronizer was taken over', the legitimate government could be brought to an end without any suspicion of the coup. The central coup had happened an indefinite time before, with the purges of minor branches of technical government following (including of the secret police). The abandondero could then with impunity torment citizens with rays, and abduct young people for torture, and kill any individuals who tried to respond to this situation. Because of the 'strangle hold on the telenews centers' no rumours of these takeovers reached the Atlans, and by 'continually checking over people's minds for any who were becoming suspicious', any resistance was averted.

This then is a technologically dependent society taken over by evil intent – subjected to folly, cruelty and exploitation – but with all the surface appearances of the original social and political life – wisdom, benignity and public good. As the invading forces penetrate the tunnels, they receive confirmation of the horrors of the hidden regime in the form of a market of human flesh. Again, Mutan reflects on the deception and lesson to be learned: 'So much for our illusion of benevolent government! How long had it been composed of hidden, grinning cannibals, the whole of our race unaware of its ultimate fate? I realized now that it takes more than patriotism and fine words over a telescreen from a ro face to make a state a safe place to live in'.

He continues his political analysis, offering some kind of summary of the lessons:

> Because of a degenerating sun, all our apparent tremendous scientific advance had been set at naught by a few madmen ... with these dero creatures eager to do anything the madmen said in return for a little fresh human meat. I saw now the fatal weakness in centralized government. One silent grab at that neck of power lines had resulted in death for the whole cream of the race. The awful power in telaug rodite methods of rule had only served to place the total wealth of the planet in mad criminal hands.

This summary is the message for future man, a paranoid message certainly, built around disgust at the human-consuming practices of the elite together with penetration behind the surface of the media-created lies which conceal these interests and practices. 'The news system had managed to ignore all such tales ... There is no cloak for corruption like the average citizen's supreme faith that all is well as long as the paper is delivered, the telenews functions without saying anything alarming, and the dignitaries strut their pompous fronts regularly as upholders of righteousness'.

Mutan's conclusions therefore juxtapose his time and ours: the revelation of the true causes of Mu's situation serves as a warning to the present reader, the descendant of the remnant left behind after the planet's evacuation, living under the same ageing sun and, who knows, under similar political conditions. He sketches out the prospects for continuing life on the surface of this planet, without protection from 'detrimental forces as well as the radioactives that cause age': these prospects are 'continual war and complete stalling of all real racial, social and individual growth' or, if not war, 'continual social troubles, famines, diseases and death'.

CHAPTER 2

Theosophy, the source of this complex world picture

Shaver's story presents a complex set of conventions, presuppositions, and ground rules. At first sight, we are offered a familiar science fiction world, with novelties that need to be spelt out together with flight between planets at the large scale and mental interaction at the more personal level. Yet there are many things that need to be explained. Setting aside the invented vocabulary which decorates the narrative, substituting unfamiliar terms for mostly familiar ideas, there is the adoption of the names for the land, Atlantis, and the planet, Lemuria, together with that of the occupants, Atlans. Then, there is an organized social hierarchy between races, one advanced and the other backward, Titans and culture men, where social distinction and separation of roles is justified by the fact that one race has the role of creator and the other of creature. The distinction between them is vast, in terms of vitality, intellect and mental powers; this appears in the authority and attractiveness of the Titans together with their technical roles and their abilities of insight and thought transference, in contrast to the limited potential of the living beings they manufacture and train. Nevertheless, the relation between them is not simply that of master and slave or owner and chattel, for, with education and dedication, the creature can gain new powers and skills and come to participate to a degree in both the plans and mental abilities of the masters, who offer suitable candidates technical direction and guidance to this end. The masters are there not simply to supervise but to teach and transform the ones they create, so that the latter may come to share some of that race's characteristics and take part in the same project. In this fashion, we find a world organized by secrets, where there is initiation into the non-obvious state of things, progress in learning and understanding, and repeated changes in perspective.

Behind this hierarchical world of social and mental relations there is a cosmology, an account of the physical world which operates at every level, from the atom to the universe, which offers a dualistic picture of cycles of matter, again at every scale from the planetary to the emission of radiation. Just as there are vital and degenerate phases of planetary life, so there are benign and noxious rays. These cycles explain the life of the solar system, its vitality and the gradual wasting both of the environment and of lives lived within it, and also the social problems confronting the actors, who have to counter the ill-effects of the cyclical stage they experience and actively shape the life of the current society, causing it to seek the next upward phase of the cycle, by shifting to another planet if necessary. Interplanetary travel becomes an essential part of such a picture: political decisions drive the fate of the races as they seek to sustain the environment or find new pastures or turn when in trouble to another planet for help. In this fashion, the link between forms of energy and the coming race is made clear, and the task of choosing the right leaders to follow and the appropriate programme highlighted. Cycles of history are placed within cycles of the life of the planetary system and, we glimpse, these placed within higher cosmic cycles of advancement and retreat. There is an interplay and correspondence between every level and scale, from the personal to the universal.

Evolution is then not an impersonal process guided by chance, but one organized with a higher aim in view, in which the enlightened actor can participate and contribute. This teleological vision is paid for by constant vigilance, which can seem like paranoia. It is expressed in various necessities: the need to choose the right leaders, to avoid the traps created by the ill-effects of radiation including their deliberate misuse, to live and act in conformity with cosmic purposes, and to navigate a world in which overhearing clues, deciphering secrets and reading the intentions of hidden hierarchies all have to be skills learnt and perfected.

I. The role of Theosophy – a summary

Where does the idea come from of a system of planets populated by intelligent forms of life? Shaver's is by no means an original picture,[1] but it presents a modern synthesis of some depth with a characteristic account of life elsewhere and its relation to earth. This account has been shared and put to work in many forms during the twentieth century, proving apt to each context. It puts together a range of ideas in a coherent structure, employed indifferently to narrate future human lives in space or encounters with life forms coming from other planets, and includes themes which one might expect: travel between planets undertaken by future men or intelligent creatures, in either case coming from civilizations on planets which display advanced technology and 'alien' culture, policies and politics. These kinds of elements come into play whenever people have considered the possibility of life elsewhere or in the future, clothing that possibility in terms borrowed from experience of present life on earth. But there are two other characteristics which demand more reflection, and which serve as signatures of the type of literature which is our concern.

The first characteristic is that exceptional mental powers are attributed to other life forms (or, equally, to future humans), powers such as the ability to read minds, to communicate without using words, to foresee future situations accurately and to predict and evaluate the outcome of actions with certainty. Along with their advanced technology and scientific knowledge, then, other life forms have psychic powers of clairvoyance and telepathy, so that they do not need to remember, analyse and predict as we do, but instead know the past, present and future with immediacy. Connected to this capacity, other life forms can maintain mutual mental communication so that they share information instantaneously, an ability they can on occasion extend to the present-day humans they encounter, both reading human intentions and sometimes engaging in telepathic communication

---

[1] There are earlier ideas of life on other planets, mapped by Crowe (1986) and Dick (1982, 1996).

with them. Rather than living, as we do, in temporal sequences where life is mapped in language, and the material and the ideal are inextricably mingled together, future or other forms of life are supposed to have separated mind from the constraints of matter and to be able to know, and to communicate, in a single moment: they deal, we might say, in undistorted information rather than in the approximations of language, and in simultaneities rather than narrative sequence or unfolding (cf. Peters 1999).

This aspect of 'mind over matter' may be the most widespread feature of the literature of science fiction. Classic instances include Stapledon, Smith, Van Vogt, Heinlein, Asimov, Herbert and Le Guin, and the theme extends to the present, shaping fiction about the Search for Extra-Terrestrial Intelligence, Artificial Intelligence and the 'Singularity'.

The second exceptional characteristic is linked to the first and is found in the concern other life forms are supposed to show for present-day human life on earth: there is a presumed symmetry between the human search for life elsewhere and the interest shown in human activity by such life forms. This feature is as surprising as the first: just as matters of 'lucidity' – clairvoyance and telepathy – should not be taken for granted, so too an acute reciprocal interest between species is not a common part of our experience. In fact, we take little interest in other creatures, intelligent or not, except to eat them, and we certainly do not expect to communicate with them.[2] In taking this symmetry of mutual interest for granted, we are assuming a central place for human understandings in the ordering of the wider universe, one that is not normally reflected in our view of nature. Where do these specific features come from?

The short answer is the idea of intelligent life on other planets derives from Theosophy, an intellectual and religious movement created in the last part of the nineteenth century. Let me lay out my case in summary form. These two features of psychic power and sympathy – along with others,

---

2   This attitude is the basis of H. G. Well's *The War of the Worlds* (1897), who does not, then, share the presuppositions I am discussing (although unusual mental properties occur in some of the short stories, e.g. 'The Remarkable Case of Davidson's Eyes', drawing on notions of the Fourth Dimension and non-Euclidean geometry – see Bergonzi 1961: 63–64). The model I propose is specific and has its limits.

such as the possibility of advanced civilizations on other planets and of travel between them – emerged in Theosophy as an expansion of spiritualist concerns. In brief, life elsewhere consists in spirits transformed, and this is a theosophical invention. And the spirit origin of alien life explains what we expect of it: it defines the affinities and capacities and limitations of these life forms.

The story of this transformation of spirit to alien visitor rests on the uses made by Madame Blavatsky, the principal author of Theosophy, of developments in contemporary physics and evolutionary biology. While Blavatsky accepted the positivist account prevalent in the 1870s and 1880s, she also had an acute eye for the vulnerability of that position, identifying specific points at which the mechanisms proposed failed to explain the phenomena being brought into view by new techniques and theories. These specific points were found both at the very large scale and the very small, as scientific research expanded the scope of space and time, causing the break-down of previously secure 'second order' categories against which new discoveries could be measured and made sense of. A series of scientific advances in the period undermined and changed understandings of the basic nature both of matter and of life. Blavatsky was sensitive to the new potentials emerging through the transformation of a manifold of commonly held ideas and exploited their possibilities to re-describe the human situation with reformist aims in mind. By no means a unique figure in the period in this regard, she sought to integrate contemporary revisions of the nature of reality with a collective, social project, intending to gain benefits for humankind from the new understanding of what is ultimately the case.

Blavatsky therefore developed a theodicy, a description of the reasons for human woes and the potential for human well-being, which worked with the extraordinary range of scales – from the expanded universe to the level of atoms – which was emerging at the time, gathering a group of followers to explore and spread her message. She created a small movement around her insight which displayed the characteristic features of such secret societies.

Spirits played a specific role within this movement and vision, acting as a link that joined the disturbances and opportunities created by the shifts in scientific categories on the one hand to human organizations and projects on the other. But the spirits were transformed to match the variety of scales at which the materials used demanded they operate. In brief, spirits acted as relays, allowing human groups to relate and to revise their relations by putting to work the alterations in potential glimpsed in the shifts in the understanding of the nature of materiality and life. The transformation of the spirits of the dead into actors at a cosmic scale created the picture of life elsewhere with which we are concerned, planetary spirits with advanced mental powers focussed upon life on Earth.

The process of transformation can be traced in detail (see the Appendix). Through such reading, we arrive at a description of the emergence of the ground rules for much science fiction, including Shaver, which is then ready to play its role as a relay in further assemblages as reports of flying saucers begin.

Within the work of this derivation, a more general point emerges. Theosophy may be considered as an example of thinking with science, or the moral employment of the effects of scientific discoveries, and it illustrates the social role of innovation in science and technology in promoting new thought. All that is well known and understood. But this instance also offers some insight into the processes by which disturbances in orders of thought are translated into social effects in the surrounding society, notably in that they demand an intermediary form of linkage, which I have called a relay – a form with an uncertain existence except that it can be perceived in its effects in human groups.

Such relays are not the passive creatures of activities taking place elsewhere in well-defined social zones: they are not simply reflections of, say, a laboratory situation. On the contrary, they have active powers; they join together, over time, the activities and thinking of hither-to unconnected human groups and may produce actions in either party which were not previously conceivable. Relays are then active forms (even if hard to represent) which produce interactions with unpredictable outcomes. Although we can connect Blavatsky's writings to innovations in the material and life sciences, these innovations themselves may be products of earlier relays and connections. In this fashion, the present essay may be thought of as exploring one stretch of a longer chain of interactions and effects, organized by relays. Without any sense of teleology or fate, the contribution of

Theosophy to the creation of science fiction is a moment in the history of flying saucers.

The Theosophical movement

The Theosophical Society was founded in New York in 1875 by a woman of Russian birth, Helena Petrovna Blavatsky (1831–1891), and an American lawyer, Henry Steel Olcott (1832–1907).[3] While the later claim is that the society was formed to promote the study of ancient wisdom and explore the ideas it contained in a practical fashion, this is to tidy up the history somewhat, for its initial focus was around the reformation and elevation of Spiritualism (Prothero 2011: 53, 62). The relation of the original impulse to the later project is central to our present concern.

The ideas that make up Theosophy can be found in Madame Blavatsky's writings, which she first laid out in *Isis Unveiled* (1877) and developed to their fullest expression in *The Secret Doctrine* (1888). She was the movement's main intellectual, while Olcott provided the ethical and organizational drive (Prothero 2011: 53). Blavatsky, however, did not work alone. In the first place, she claimed to be the amanuensis and pupil of occult teachers, called variously Adepts, Brothers, Masters and Mahatmas, who not only had instructed her in the past but gave her sight of documents to copy, dictated texts to her, corrected and supplemented her writings, and offered instruction and answered questions with both direct mental and written communications, leaving behind many, sometimes substantial, letters, some of which are now in the possession of the British Library (see Barker 1924). These sources are disputed, but the motif of secret teaching is a standard

---

3   The history of the movement has been well discussed. For recent biographies, see Meade (1980), Cranston (1993), and Johnson (1994) on Blavatsky, and Prothero (2011) on Olcott. For an introduction to Theosophy, see Campbell (1980). Godwin (2013) provides a summary of the first generation of Theosophists; Godwin (1994) and Washington (1993) place Theosophy in a broader history. Hammer and Rothstein (2013) offer a thorough coverage of the various figures and successive generations.

trope in the period, with many memoires and novels claiming to transcribe a source or to record the genius of another actor, or even to be the expression of a mind other than the author's. Meade mentions the novelist Bulwer-Lytton, the spiritualist Emma Hardinge Britten, and the spirit-scribe Andrew Jackson Davis as instances familiar to Blavatsky (Meade 1980: 163).[4] From the last, she would also have gained an acquaintance with Fourier's and, especially, Swedenborg's ideas – the latter being Davis's source while in mesmeric rapport (Albanese 2007: 208–229).

In the second place, Blavatsky read widely, using contemporary scholarly syntheses and collections of sources, but also showing acquaintance with original sources; critics traced these borrowings with philological enthusiasm (see Coleman's appendix in Solovyov 1895). Then, while writing both her major works, she created a team around her who supplied materials and arranged, typed, edited and corrected her productions, which she then further developed at the galley and page proof stages. This process was in evidence in writing both major works; *The Secret Doctrine* was in some regards a collective work, produced by a team of pupils (see Meade 1980: 382, 395, 406), while Olcott gives extensive evidence on his and others' contributions to *Isis Unveiled* (see Zirkoff 1972: 20, 55). Last, in certain instances followers claimed to draw on the same teachers and sources as Blavatsky who, in the early cases, mediated the transmission of messages and letters: Sinnett, Leadbeater and Besant all represent examples.

Blavatsky wrote many letters and articles in addition to her published books and was the subject of controversy in personal letters and in print; these together provide most of the materials for the histories and biographies.[5] Just as with spirits and with flying saucers, there is a well-defined series of reported incidents and sources, subject to both contemporary and

---

4   For Bulwer-Lytton, see Liljegren (1957); for the Britten connection, see Godwin (1994: 200–206).
5   Sinnett (1886), Solovyov (1895) and Olcott (1875, 1972–1975) provide a good deal of the primary material for the biographies. Solovyov contains testimony from Blavatsky's sister, Madame Jelihowski. The memoire by her cousin, Count Witte (1921), also contains a much-cited account of Blavatsky's early years, although not from a contemporary.

subsequent debates; Theosophy is an example of a movement which wrote itself into existence through a sequence of communications and disputes. And, just as with spirits and flying saucers, Blavatsky divided and continues to divide opinion along well-recognized options: were things as she claimed, beginning with her sources and proceeding to their teaching, or was she a fraud, even if one of genius, and her followers credulous and deceived? How the questions are answered may have practical consequences, so they are not negligible; however, neither alternative exhausts the interest of Madame Blavatsky. Whatever their source, her writings and the movement which bore (and bears) witness to them had their own forms of existence and participated in the world, and part of this life – the part which concerns us – included giving the ground-rules for much of the science fiction genre. These ground-rules, however, were given inadvertently; to understand how this form arose and to grasp its attraction, we will look, first, at Blavatsky's relationship to Spiritualism and, second, at her engagements with contemporary scientific thought, and show how, by bringing the two aspects together, she transformed this relationship into a wider cosmology, one which, among other results, distributes spirits to other planets as well as this.

II. Blavatsky's relationship to Spiritualism

Theosophy developed out of Spiritualism; Spiritualism – and not Asian religion – was the foundation and key to Blavatsky's extraordinary synthesis. Her early career can be reconstructed, although it must be with care, for we rely for the most part on Blavatsky's retrospective accounts in letters and interviews, together with recollections and reminiscences from the memoires of contemporaries, and the settling of accounts by former followers and friends.[6] While these parties all had interests of one

---

6   I rely for this historical sketch on the recent biographies listed in note 3, although I have also looked at the sources mentioned in note 5 on which the biographies draw.

kind and another, nevertheless, the resulting biography bears the characteristic marks both of a medium's self-narrative and of a typical medium's history.

In Blavatsky's case, we have a childhood marked by imaginary playmates, visions of people at moments of crisis and of nature spirits, states of altered consciousness, and invisible guardians; she also received communications by spirit writing. Her apprenticeship as a medium developed during the period between her leaving her family in Russia in 1849, at the age of 17, and her emigration to the United States in 1873. This was the period when Spiritualism was introduced and spread in Europe, expanding in circles with a pre-existing interest in metaphysical matters touching on religious, scientific and political innovation; such circles included the upper-class Russian social milieu from which Blavatsky had emerged and to which she tended to gravitate in each foreign centre she visited (for background see Young 2012). Blavatsky travelled from Constantinople to Cairo in 1850 as companion to a reputed medium. She made the acquaintance in Paris in 1858 of the famous medium Daniel Home through his Russian wife. When she returned to her Russian family later that year, there is testimony to her growing mediumistic powers, producing raps in answer to questions and poltergeist effects, evidence of thought reading and the ability to discern illnesses, and physical effects such as delivering letters written by spirits and automatic writing (Sinnett 1886; cf. Solovyov 1895; Cranston 1993: 65–69). While Blavatsky later discriminated between the effects she produced and those attributable either to spirits or to ghosts and poltergeists, crediting her own to 'beings [mortals] know nothing about', the repertoire developed owed everything to the Spiritualism of the period. After more than a decade of further travel, she can be traced in Cairo in 1871, sharing lodgings with a medium with who she organized a brief-lived 'society for the investigation of spiritualistic phenomena ... based on the doctrines of Allan Kardec' (Meade 1980: 94); she returned to Paris via Odessa in 1873, again mixing in spiritualist circles, and then moved to New York in June 1873.

Once in New York, her life becomes better documented, for she began a career as both a writer and a public medium and she shaped her life story, becoming a self-created, though contested, figure; there are contemporary reports of her presence at séances, interviews and, in due course, polemics both against her claims and in her defence in spiritualist papers and the local press. In short, she moved in spiritualist circles, held séances and demonstrated clairvoyant powers. She met Olcott in Chittenden, Vermont, while visiting the Eddy brothers, mediums who materialized spirits, and she participated in their séances. Olcott wrote an enthusiastic account[7] which was subsequently challenged in the press and the Eddys denounced as frauds, and Blavatsky wrote in defence of the phenomena, announcing herself as 'a Spiritualist of many years' standing'. This episode (recounted in Meade 1980: 104–130; cf. Cranston 1993: 123–129) is exemplary for its combination of elements: the production of spirit phenomena cannot be separated from either the element of performance for an audience or from the reception of the audience's reports. The reports were received and judged in both the spiritualist and public press, one group maintaining the reality of the phenomena encountered (and advancing a variety of theories 'explaining' the events witnessed), the other offering a different account, usually charging the mediums with fraud and the witnesses with credulity. The several parties – spirits, mediums, witnesses, advocates, critics, and the amplifying presence of the publishing media – cannot be separated into primary sources and secondary (and tertiary) accounts: incidents, reports and debates are inextricably bound up together in what we may call rhetorical events, constructed around attempts at persuasion, instances in which the parties involved advocate and embody competing 'worldviews'. Public mediumship cannot then be separated from polemic: it consists not in 'facts' but in testimony, in appeals to notions of 'independent confirmation' and in challenges to the evidence. The ground-rules employed by each side (relating to distinct notions of belief, language and experience) remain incompatible, and the minutiae of the evidence appealed to in these quarrels bear witness to their irresolvable nature.

At the end of 1874, Blavatsky moved to Philadelphia, where she participated in another famous spiritualist scandal, the imposition by a pair of mediums named Holmes on the elderly Robert Dale Owen, creating for him a materialized spirit called Katie King. Once again, Blavatsky defended

[7] His collected articles were published as Olcott (1875).

the Holmes' claims, organizing materialization séances for Olcott's benefit and claiming to be visited by Katie's father, the spirit John King, who acted as control for several mediums in the period (Cranston 1993: 130–133).

Within eighteen months of her arrival in the States, Blavatsky had then settled into the East Coast spiritualist milieu and was writing for spiritualist journals, organizing séances and producing phenomena. She also began to develop her thinking within this framework, in part seeking to distinguish herself and Olson from the moral backwardness and philosophical naivety of the spiritualist movement (Prothero 2011: 44). The spirit John King became both a protector to her and the messenger of a secret group, a brotherhood of living men – not spirits – based in Egypt, consisting of a leader and seven associates or Masters. This group had elected her to be its spokesman and to carry its message – its teachings concerning the secrets of the Universe – to the human race. This group called itself 'the Brotherhood of Luxor', taking the title from a pamphlet Olcott had written (see Meade 1980: 138–147). In this fashion, Blavatsky began her move from the role of a medium to that of an 'ethical and religious teacher', drawing on the occult tradition and on ancient wisdom. While spirits produced in séances became rejected as the misunderstood effects of a larger system, Blavatsky retained her clairvoyant and other powers, because these phenomena became evidence of the presence of the unseen beings which communicated with and through her. She and Olcott formed the Theosophical Society in 1875 to explore these powers and to study the wisdom to which they bore witness.

She also wrote an account of this system of learning that was being revealed to her, *Isis Unveiled*, published in 1877. It forms one of a series of revelations made to the American people during the nineteenth century: The *Book of Mormon*, Davis's Harmonial Philosophy, and – contemporary to Blavatsky's writing – Oahspe, the Kosmon Bible, produced by automatic typewriting in 1881.[8]

---

8   For the first two, see Albanese (2007), for the last, Kripal (2011: 109).

The ideas motivating Spiritualism

What 'adhesions' (Tylor) do the notion of spirits bring with them? This is important, because their inheritance is passed on to their progeny, both Masters and visitors from space. Moore (1977) has identified three broad strands of ideas at work in the spiritualist movement, beneath the surface of surprising phenomena. The first is the employment of scientific ideas to moral ends, exploiting disturbances created by contemporary scientific discoveries and technological innovations in the wider realm of common thought. Spiritualism specifically engages with longer-term meditations on ideas of 'action at a distance' derived from Newton's writings (and transmitted through mesmerist concerns), then, the recent invention of the telegraph, considered as a means of communication over distance, and later, discussions around the 'law of the conservation of energy'.[9] Together, these supported such possibilities as the direct mental intuition of realities, communication between disembodied minds, and the transformation (rather than loss) of souls after bodily death.

But there was another, equally important strand to this kind of thinking, the motive of reform: purifying practitioners' lives and deepening their self-understanding. As Braude points out, Spiritualism arose as part of a spectrum of movements arising from the collapse of Calvinist certainties and given form as the Second Great Awakening, in a geography and milieu marked by revival and impulses towards social reform. Early Spiritualism pivoted around the Quaker notion of 'inner light' (or direct communication), expressed in personal and political reform (Braude 2001: chapter 1).[10] In writing about Theosophy, two generations later, Prothero identifies these reformist aims as characteristic of contemporary liberal Protestant ambitions concerning self-making – the moral and intellectual formation

---

9   The law of conservation of energy, though formulated by the early 1850s, only entered popular consciousness in the 1870s (see Elkana 1974: 191).
10 We should note the ambiguity inherent in the notion of reform, with its focus on articulating the wrongs of the present society and far less detailed visions of a new age. Reynolds (1988: 85) points to 'the relativism implied by this fluid reform environment' of the 1840s.

of the self – summing up its ethos as 'its critique of Calvinist predestination in the name of individual liberty, its anticlericalism and emphasis on vernacular preaching by the laity, its antidogmatism and exaltation of individual conscience, its attempt to improve the role of women in society, and, finally, its hope of fashioning something akin to the kingdom of God on earth' (Prothero 2011: 53).

The religious and political categories of reform at work in this broad movement cannot be separated from the tropes linking the physical world and the potential of the mind: they construct a single manifold of possibilities. The question is: how are they joined? This is the role of the third strand, which concerns the form of the spiritualist revision of Christian ideas about human survival after death, focussed on the possibility of family members (particularly infants) continuing to live after death and to communicate with the living.

Braude points out that the loss of friends and family members, especially of children, became felt in a new way in the context of the Second Great Awakening and the new Evangelical emphasis on self-making and 'the role of human agency in the drama of salvation' (Braude 2001: 50). Once humans had become responsible for the act of conversion, rather than leaving this matter in the hands of God, and could be held accountable, this placed new emphasis upon the moment of death for, up to that point, an unregenerate person was capable of repentance. The moment of death then became a focus of anxiety, which 'became acute in the case of infants and children, who died before they had an opportunity to exercise their own agency towards conversion' (Braude 2001: 51).

Braude also indicates shifts in the social and working environment that accompanied this change: an increasing distinction of the domestic sphere from that of work, and the growing separation of the sexes between the two, so that death, and particularly the death of children, became the concern of women and of men reconciled to the new style of domesticity. At the same time, images of heaven became modelled on new ideals of suburban life, as did burial grounds, reflecting this separation of home and work, and the notion arose in evangelical preaching of death as a home-coming (Braude 2001: 52). We may add, Spiritualism spread not because of the success of public mediums, about which we have abundant materials, but because of the development of 'home circles', family groups, together with a few close friends, for which we have few sources. These groups were concerned to contact close relations, especially children and infants who had died, to sustain reciprocal relations of care and companionship (cf. Owen 2004a).

Spiritualist practices developed in this context characterized by the collapse of Calvinist ideas concerning death, the emergence of modern notions of social and personal agency, and a new division of responsibilities between the sexes. Andrew Jackson Davis's influential contribution, according to Braude, was to articulate 'a comprehensive worldview incorporating spirit manifestations, reform principles, and an anti-Calvinist theology into a single system' (Braude 2001: 35). And Spiritualism came at the far end of a spectrum of Liberal Christian positions that rejected ideas of inherent human sinfulness, the salvation of only an elect few, and the condemnation of the disobedient majority to endless suffering in hell.[11]

Spiritualists did not need to rely on either speculation or revelation to deny these doctrines, for they gained testimony to the afterlife from the spirits through the séance, and this account confirmed such principles as the benignity of Nature and its purposes, and its progress towards (in Davis's words) 'true fraternal harmony' (Braude 2001: 36). The spirits returned to reassure the living as to their fate and confirmed the image of heaven as a 'summer-land' where the individual's development continued after death and relationships were sustained. And the spirits gave account of their ability to pass from one state of life to another, to travel at will and to communicate directly in accordance with the possibilities of the latest scientific discoveries. There are many contemporary testimonies, particularly from women, as to the relief granted by spiritualist experiences, freeing the living from fear of a vengeful God and from the notion of punishment inflicted on those who had, for whatever reason, not been able to commit to their Saviour in this life.

As part of a spectrum of liberal churches and reformist movements, spiritualists could then make a new accommodation with a 'scientific' view of Nature. They shared a good deal with Transcendentalism, making

---

11 Her sources are Ahlstrom (1972: chapter 25), Haroutunian (1932) and Farrell (1980).

both 'liberal theology and transcendental visions widely available' (Braude 2001: 46), and they drew followers from such Christian movements as Unitarians, Universalists, and Quakers. At the same time, the possibility of new life was associated with visions of social repair. Spiritualists participated in a variety of reformist movements such as abolitionism, temperance, vegetarianism, the reform of marriage, of labour relations, of dress and of health (Braude 2001: 3). But their special contribution was the development of a detailed picture of life after death, not only offering 'concrete descriptions of lost loved ones after death', but also an account of 'progression', 'asserting that individual souls continued to grow in grace after death, advancing through a series of successively more perfect spheres, each suited to promote spiritual development for the attainment of the next sphere of heaven. Andrew Jackson Davis's revelations (drawing on Swedenborg's scheme) developed a series of six celestial spheres of increasing harmony, beauty and wisdom through which the soul advances after death' (Braude 2001: 40). This moral vision was an incitement to advancement through the successive spheres, a model of salvation based in gradual maturation and progress, and not in the abrupt nature of death and judgement.

We may sum up the questions of spiritualist motivations as follows. Scientific discoveries and technological innovations caused repeated disturbances and adjustments in basic categories concerning the nature of matter and the underlying order of reality. These alterations and the new possibilities they indicated were in turn put to work in various attempts to repair things perceived to be going badly in the surrounding society, whether within the family or in wider settings, encompassing a wide range of interventions, reforming relations between the sexes, generations, classes and races, together with habits, mores and other directly political and economic arrangements. And the relay between these shifts in the collective mental order on the one hand and projects of reform on the ground on the other was effected by newly-conceived agents, the spirits of the dead, permitted by the first kind and assisting, even enabling, the second. Spirits bore within them a range of capacities linked to new technical and scientific properties and modelling them, capacities of perception, communication and intervention, explaining their powers of lucidity and abilities to heal and repair. As recent members of the living, now on a higher plane, they were also animated by the desire to assist humanity. They then join the psychic qualities and the human focus we noted at the outset as requiring some explanation. And they carried over these powers and affinity when they were put to new work, as they were when taken up in Blavatsky's concerns.

Blavatsky's later history

Olcott's and Blavatsky's relationship evolved, beginning with their mutual interest in spirits and in the reform of Spiritualism, and proceeding to their respective roles in the production of the text of *Isis Unveiled*, shaped, if not precisely by spirits, by communications from unseen beings. These beings operated within the spirit conventions of the period, working through mental messages, second sight, written letters, producing various physical objects and even, on occasion, materializations, making a visitation in visible form. Although Theosophy in part defined itself against the immoral practices of some mediums and, at the same time, against the widespread lack of understanding of the phenomena in which spiritualists dealt, its main motive was the shared one of reform: applying the motive of reform reflexively to the spiritualist movement to purify practitioners' lives and deepen their learning.[12]

Prothero distinguishes between ante- and post-Bellum forms of this broad impulse to reform (drawing on McLoughlin 1978), contrasting the universal, optimistic, individualistic and anti-institutional, overtly religious tendencies of the earlier version, with its 'millennialism, voluntarism, and perfectionism' (Prothero 2011: 17), and the more secular progressive reformism of the later period, with lower horizons of ambition, tempered by the experience of conflict. Certainly, Spiritualism changed a good deal from the 1850s to the 1870s and, as it struggled to establish its credentials by engaging with each new technical means – particularly photography and voice recording – to offer material proofs of the spirits' presence, it may have become open to Olcott's charges of having a low philosophical

---

12 This point is important given the effort by later theosophical writers such as Zirkoff (1972) to distinguish Blavatsky's work in *Isis Unveiled* from spiritualist practices.

content, being puerile and repulsive, and embracing the fallacies of free love and individual sovereignty (in an article in 1875, cited by Meade 1980: 150).

Blavatsky and Olcott represented distinct paths to spiritualist reform. Blavatsky used the paraphernalia and practices of Spiritualism to investigate the sources to which she believed Spiritualism pointed but had neither understood nor mastered: she was concerned to develop a metaphysical cosmology which would allow development of individual powers of lucidity and supernormal action. Olcott, on the contrary, although drawn in by these concerns, quickly turned to a project of social reform of the Asian religions along liberal Protestant lines – this is Prothero's central thesis (see Prothero 2011: 69) – drawing on a synthetic core of 'original' Eastern teaching to found the possibility of a universal brotherhood, and working to create institutions to that end. In Olcott's reform, his Buddhism resembled contemporary liberal Protestant concerns by focussing on scripture and rejecting ritual, criticizing such orthodox Christian doctrines as miracles, incarnation, heaven and hell, and looking to personal moral reform as the key to religion, distrusting clerical and traditional authority and emphasizing the importance of reason and experience. In short, he believed in salvation by moral example and imitation, buttressed by social reform, advocating such contemporary concerns as education, anti-slavery, temperance, chastity and women's rights (see Prothero 2011: 104).

Olcott then increasingly turned his back on Blavatsky's magical focus, in part because of its potential to discredit his reformist alliances. On the other hand, he could draw on her remarkable synthesis and portrayal of an original core of religious teachings for his projects. They therefore had a way to travel together and, indeed, despite disagreements, never broke with one another. Their interest in Eastern wisdom and teachers took them to India early in 1879, where Olcott had already established contact with Indian reformers.

In India, Blavatsky made the acquaintance of Alfred Sinnett (1840–1921), who edited an English-language daily newspaper published in Allahabad. She impressed Sinnett and Olcott with a sequence of phenomena leading to direct communications from the Masters, a series to which Sinnett bore witness in *The Occult World* (published in 1881). She first produced raps and materialized flowers as evidence of the physical powers of the astral body of a distant 'Brother' or Adept (Sinnett 1969: 46), preparing for the communication of letters from the same source, the arrival of which was signalled by a bell, comparable to a telegraphic call-bell (Sinnett 1969: 51). The visiting Adept also offered more substantial signs, producing an extra teacup and saucer required on a picnic, a bottle of water, and a brooch which had been lost elsewhere and which was returned, repaired. These phenomena have been much discussed. Sinnett twice remarks on the similarity of these phenomena to conjuring tricks (Sinnett 1969: 65, 80f.),[13] but distinguishes the motives of the parties responsible in either instance, as well as testifying to the difficulty of subjecting either Madame Blavatsky or the Brothers to testing. The book is full of further incidents, including physical appearances by the Masters, as well as discussions preparing for their wider teachings. The incidents are marked by a certain triviality, well characterized by William James' general remark concerning psychic phenomena: 'These experiences have three characters in common: they are capricious, discontinuous, and not easily controlled; they require peculiar persons for their production; and their significance seems to be solely for personal life' (quoted in Gauld 1968: 354). Yet despite their small-scale focus, the implications of the teachings are, by contrast, wide-reaching. Persuaded by these phenomena, Sinnett asked Blavatsky to transmit a letter from him to the Brothers using her form of 'psychological telegraph' (Sinnett 1969: 83), asking for proofs, leading to a correspondence which Sinnett published in 1883 as *Esoteric Buddhism* (Sinnett 1972).

In a repeat of Blavatsky's history in Philadelphia, her forms of demonstration became the subject first of published testimony and then of dispute; there was controversy around each sign or incident. When she returned with Olcott to London in 1884, the Theosophical Society became an object of interest to the recently formed Society for Psychical Research. This enquiry was extended because Blavatsky's practices in India came under scrutiny due to an accomplice's betrayal of secrets in her absence (for the Coulomb affair, see Coulomb 1885; Meade 1980: 335–345 and passim.; Cranston 1993: 261–297), leading to an investigation conducted by Richard

---

[13] Stage conjuring developed in parallel with Spiritualism in this period, reproducing the phenomena of the séance – see Steinmeyer (2005); cf. Jones (2017).

Hodgson at the Theosophists' headquarters at Adyar which resulted in a report denouncing her as a fraud (Society for Psychical Research 1885). By the time of this setback she had moved permanently back to Europe, after a second, relatively short, visit to India to organize an answer to her critics. She then lived in a series of European countries, meeting Solovyov, first a follower, then a critic and a source for this period (see Solovyov 1895), when in Paris, and settled finally in London, where she responded to the crisis of Hodgson's report, as she had after the first scandals in America, by producing another major synthesis, *The Secret Doctrine* (1888). She died in 1891.

III. Thinking with science

If spirits act as relays, how did their task evolve in Blavatsky's writings and, particularly, in *The Secret Doctrine*? She put the latest scientific advances to work to render plausible an account of the cosmos and the place of man within it, drawing new theories of the nature of matter, of the history of the earth and the planets, of the development of life, and of evidence of human progress into a single narrative. In the broadest terms, the striking feature of the new discoveries concerned the expansion of scale above or below that of human experience: the magnitude of the universe, the minute dimensions of the atoms and molecules constituting matter and life, and the immense periods of time needed to account for the evolution of the universe, of life within it, and of mankind. The interest lies in how Blavatsky employs these discoveries of scale and the openings they offer to the work of spirits.[14]

Blavatsky engaged in detail with contemporary scholarship; her reading was prodigious. A mark of her intelligence is that she was sensitive

---

14   Noakes (2019) gives a detailed account of the interpenetration of Spiritualism and scientific thinking in the period, but from a different angle; although theosophists are discussed, there is no consideration of Blavatsky's specific contribution and reading.

to the points at which recent discoveries brought into question presuppositions which had allowed previous syntheses to work. In this fashion, without necessarily grasping the direction of travel of the new work, she was able to criticize features of established sciences where the underlying categories were shifting. She achieved this effect with respect to physical phenomena by identifying issues both at the level of molecular activity and at the cosmological scale when the regularities identified by Newtonian mechanics broke down. With respect to biological processes, she employed the same approach: identifying limits or lacunae regarding the mechanisms of selection and heredity at the small scale and, at the large scale, seizing on the failure to explain high level patterns such as speciation, the distinct body plans of phyla, or the division into the animal and vegetable kingdoms. Without a grasp on the inner logic of the natural scientific arguments, she had an intuitive sense of where the proposed mechanisms of mechanics and natural selection cease to operate, or come into question, as a means of explanation or a principle of intelligibility. We will look at the evidence for this claim below.

She was then what Ardener (2007) has called a 'prophet': a person who deals not in predictions of the future but who discerns shifts in contemporary definitional space, who grasps a mutation in the second-order categories, by which I mean the categories against which we measure novelties to make sense of them, and who reads social significance into these alterations. Blavatsky put these discernments with respect to the uneven progress of the modern sciences to work to serve a theodicy, explaining human woes and well-being and offering a guide to right action, and constructed a cosmology and anthropology from the scientific materials as an expression of this theodicy. In both physical and biological spheres, she sought to show that the motivations for development were not random and externally generated, but internally sourced and purposeful. Crucially, she argued that the break-down of mechanistic or materialist explanations points to the presence of intentional action behind the processes, and serves as evidence for spirit activity, organized and integrated by a Cosmic Mind. In this fashion, the work of spirits was extended far beyond its original compass and applied to organizing the Universe at every scale.

Continuities and innovations in the categories of the physical sciences

Let us look further (though in modest detail) at Blavatsky's engagement with, first, the physical sciences, in Part III (The Addenda) of Book I of *The Secret Doctrine* (Blavatsky 1999, I: 477–676). She offers a review of the major theoretical innovations of nineteenth-century physics which, if we follow Harman, may be summarized in the ideas of energy, force and matter: the principles of the conservation and dissipation of energy, the theory of the physical 'field', accounting for the transmission of force by means of the mediating action of the medium between bodies, and the study of matter in terms of molecular physics. In a sentence, she was committed to the newly articulated 'mechanical view of nature, which supposed that matter in motion was the basis of all physical phenomena' (Harman 1982: 2). She begins with discussions around the propagation of light, favouring wave theory over the older corpuscular account. She notes the extension of mechanical explanation to the 'imponderables' of eighteenth-century physics, heat, light, magnetism, electricity and gravity, evoking ether as the medium or field through which energy is transmitted, identified both as the source of the various forces and as allowing the possibility of transformations between forms, and incorporating in this fashion the law of the conservation of energy. She next turns to the minute scale of atomic theory, with atoms conceived as centres of force, and, last, to the vast operations of nebular theory, touching on the way on the kinetic theory of gases, the interconversion of heat and matter, and the classification of the elements. It is an extraordinary circumspection which we might sum up as being concerned above all with the longstanding problem of action at a distance – or how do bodies act on one another across space? – conceived however in terms borrowed from models of intentional action or the influence of one person may have on another.[15]

For it must be remarked immediately that she adopts this mechanical view of nature for her own ends; while she may be said to have taken 'the

---

15 For a history of action at a distance, see Hesse (1962), cf. Peters (1999: 177–178); for intentional action, see Barrow (1986).

law of the conservation of energy as a unifying principle and mechanical explanation as the programme of physical theory' (Harman 1982: 2), she neglects the aims of quantification and the research for mathematical laws which gave the programme its coherence and powers of explanation, and in so doing, she also ignores the three-way distinction made in the period between mathematical description, physical models, and the real processes they claimed to represent. At the same time, she was unaware of the dialectical, experimental and provisional nature of this scientific work and the fashion in which, repeatedly, it overturned common sense categories; indeed, she defends the priority of models deriving from common sense (Blavatsky 1999, I: 488). This approach fits, then, with what we may call the poetry of literalism that she shares with Bulwer-Lytton rather than the emerging 'logic of scientific discovery'.

What then is she doing? Blavatsky take the disputes between scientists and rival theories not as the normal conditions for the construction of provisional scientific understanding, but as evidence of confusion and a symptom of the need for a supplementary level of explanation, a level that will reconcile these incompatible findings, taken as literal products. Formalizations are taken as realities, and the transformations they allow are then taken to need further explanation. The debate between the wave and corpuscular theories in the explanation of the propagation of light is exemplary in this regard; these are what she calls '*affections* of matter itself', further claiming that 'light, heat, magnetism, electricity and gravity … were not the final *causes* of the visible phenomena, including planetary motion, but themselves the Secondary *effects of other Causes* …' (Blavatsky 1999, I: 484). In this fashion, she offers a challenge to the trinity of '*Inert Matter, Senseless Force* and *Blind Chance*' (Blavatsky 1999, I: 505).

While she takes energy or force as the central organizing principle of the universe, she identifies this principle with 'life' (there is no inorganic matter, she states – Blavatsky 1999, I: 507) because the supplementary feature demanded by scientific controversy is a need to explain, on the one hand, motivation or direction (telos) and, on the other, form, in the sense of order, repetition and elegance. The mechanical account of nature, which she may have adopted with enthusiasm largely because of its antagonism to conventional Christian expression, lacks in her view any account of direction of development and order. She reads the controversies repeatedly to this end, shrewdly focussing on the very large-scale and the very small, raising the problems that emerge in the ordering of the planets by attraction and repulsion, on the one hand, and, on the other, the structure of atoms, resolved in the period by Thompson into supposed vortices and implicated in emerging theories of electromagnetic radiation. Indeed, the nineteenth-century 'settlement' of the mechanical view of nature never achieved a point of stability and was in this period being challenged by ether and field theories at the points Blavatsky had sensed (cf. Harman 1982, chapter IV).

Two outcomes emerge from her exploration of the limits of the conception of nature as matter in motion, limits conceived in terms of a lack of explanation of direction (or motivation) and form (or structure). In the first place, it enables Blavatsky to integrate the findings of modern science with the traditions of ancient wisdom, which is the ostensible purpose of the Addenda – titled 'Science and The Secret Doctrine Contrasted'. The modern sciences are rediscovering the findings of ancient wisdom, she claims, but lack its metaphysics. 'Science cannot ... unveil the mystery of the universe around us. Science can ... collect, clarify, and generalize upon phenomena; but the occultist, arguing from admitted metaphysical data, declares that the daring explorer, who would probe the innermost secrets of Nature, must transcend the narrow limitations of sense, and transfer his consciousness into the region of noumena and the sphere of primal causes ... he must develop faculties that are absolutely dormant ... in the constitution of ... our present ... race ... He can in no other conceivable manner collect the facts on which to base his speculations' (Blavatsky 1999, I: 477–478). By linking ancient wisdom to the new sciences and identifying the need for supplementary insight, she also allows the anticipation of such future sciences as the physics of the 'Coming Force', derived from Bulwer-Lytton's 'vril' and linked to a long discussion of a perpetual motion machine (Blavatsky 1999, I: 554–566), and a metaphysical chemistry of elements (Blavatsky 1999, I: 566–578), both to be discerned by a sixth sense trained beyond the five physical senses. By this last idea, she instantiates the repeated scientific break with the common-sense world in her own fashion.

In the second place, these discernments allow her to explain the processes identified in terms of the acts of 'conscious Powers and Spiritual Entities ... terrestrial, semi-intelligent, and highly intellectual Forces on other planes; and ... Beings that dwell around us in spheres, imperceptible, whether through telescope or microscope' (Blavatsky 1999, I: 478). This is Swedenborg revived (as Blavatsky observes on the last pages of Book II). The observed structures and forms of life demand a hierarchy of intentional beings, operating at many scales. Materialism misses this second level, whence, Blavatsky claims, the confusions and conflicts of the physicists. This account could allow a chaotic worldview, with no rhyme or reason governing the motive intelligences. Yet Blavatsky does not exploit the existence of theoretical conflicts in this way, but instead draws on the contemporary direction of travel towards the 'completeness of physical explanation' (cf. Papineau 2002) and posits a Cosmic Mind in which these levels of intelligent life find their order and meaning. We find evidence of 'Movers, the Intelligences within the Cosmic Soul' (Blavatsky 1999, I: 530), whether we are considering the ordering of the solar system or the construction of elements in the forms of isotopes.

Geological and biological evolution

If we turn to the Addenda to Book II (Blavatsky 1999, II: 645–798), we find similar broad patterns in Blavatsky's engagement with the geological and biological sciences. While Book I, focussing on 'Cosmogenesis', takes the developments and limits of nineteenth-century physics as its foil, Book II, concerned with 'Anthropogenesis', is constructed around a debate with Darwin's *The Decent of Man* (1871), against a backdrop of developments in the concept of geological time. Book I gives several of the cards to be played in Book II, such as directed evolution, the expansion of distance and of time, and the issue of structure at every scale in the expanded range, while Book II introduces the concept of cycles or rounds, including races within this pattern, and of evolution as an unfolding of potential contained in prototypes. Once again, the problem for the reader is to discern the sense or direction of the argument amongst the extraordinary range of theories and details of material covered.

Blavatsky deploys her reading of contemporary geological and palaeontological disputes to make several points. First, the history of the earth serves as a source for the history of the planets (see Blavatsky 1999, II: 700f.), and the contribution of the moon is particularly instructive in this regard. In both these claims, she anticipates trends in conventional geology and cosmology (see Rudwick 2014, chapter 11), although her reasoning is quite different: for her, the planets each undergo the same complex but regular guided cycle of development, and the moon in particular plays an unconventional role in the earth's development (see, e.g. Blavatsky 1999, I: 170ff.).

Second, she draws on two major trends present in nineteenth-century geological debates, the extraordinary expansion of the timescale at issue (given absolute form only in the twentieth century with radiometric dating), and a growing understanding of the event-filled nature of earth's history, exploiting the record of contingencies contained in the sequence of rock formations. In characteristic fashion, she reconciles the debate between uniformitarian claims – that physical causes at present in operation may explain geological structures from any period – and catastrophist theories – supposing periodic interruptions to regular processes (such as mass extinctions) – by positing an immensely long time-perspective in which successive world stages replace one another in an orderly succession, although interrupted by periods of chaos. In adopting such a long timescale, she draws support from cosmologists' challenges to geologists' estimates (e.g. Blavatsky 1999, II: 796); further, she uses catastrophes for even more radical purposes than their geological advocates.

Third, she exploits the fossil record to support her proposal of an orderly succession of stages, challenging the purposelessness of the mechanism of natural selection and interposing the work of active guiding spirits. And fourth, she integrates into this narrative an account of the descent of man quite at variance with the Darwinian account of man's relation to the higher mammals and the apes.

If I have presented these topics schematically in a conventional order, in descending order of scale and antiquity, Blavatsky reverses the order of presentation, playing her trumps first: the 'addenda' begin with questions of the appropriate anthropological method, followed by considering contemporary theories of the descent of man, and a review of the fossil evidence arguing for common ancestry between men and apes. She then turns to geological periods and the rise and fall of continents, linking these to the known history of the human race and introducing the possibility of yet earlier forms of humankind, together with questions of order and purpose in these successions. She concludes with the ordering of the planets. What is the purpose of this reversal?

In each chapter of this last part, she begins with polemic, taking rival scientific theories as instances of partial perspectives on an ultimately knowable state which, taken in the round, may be understood as both stable and permanent. The evidence can then be reconciled by identifying unifying concepts and adopting a method of approach which allows the investigator to pass to and fro between data and ground-rules, in conformity with the example of the contemporary positivist project, which postulated a narrative of continuous progress as 'ever more adequate unifying conceptions ... specify ever more fundamental laws' (Macintyre 1990: 20). However, rather than supposing impersonal laws and imposing coherence through the endeavours of scientists, Blavatsky has recourse to the notion of creative intelligences of a non-human kind giving form to the processes under consideration. This distinction allows several other reversals or inversions in ordering the evidence. Once she has established this initial ground, each chapter tends to fall away in a long tail of miscellaneous illustration, which hangs together only through the work of the presumed spirits.

In her perspective, evolution has a direction, contained in the earliest forms and realized over time through a determined course of development. Her theory was close (in the jargon of the period) to that of 'orthogenesis', with development 'directed along a single path by forces originating within the organisms themselves' (Bowler 1992: 7); while she rejected notions of theistic evolution as too orderly and natural selection as incoherent, she could adopt rival accounts of acquired characteristics and mutations in form as required. Contemporary Darwinism saw evolution as an irregular process, controlled by external environmental factors and continuous in the sense of a steady accumulation of small changes; Blavatsky in contrast saw the process as patterned, as inwardly – in the sense of immaterially – directed, and as capable therefore of discontinuities or leaps. These were the topics on which she confronted evolutionary theory.

Blavatsky then clearly separates herself from Darwin on the disputed topic of the transformation of species, seeing (as she put it) the progress of man as distinct from the progress of molluscs (she prefaces Book II with a quotation from *Isis Unveiled* to this effect – see Blavatsky 1999, II: xvi). And she asks, what causes variation, and what is the source of necessity over contingencies? Notions of selection by external causes 'offer no real explanation … of the "coherence" of the "ancestral types" which served as the *starting point* for physical development' (Blavatsky 1999, II: 648).

Moreover, she points to weaknesses in the theory of natural selection concerning speciation and the development of the divisions between classes of mammals, again tracing the influence of presiding spirits and the realization of astral prototypes (see Blavatsky 1999, II: 734–738).

The culmination of the argument concerns the descent of man. Blavatsky's claim is that the progressive evolution of man is the central purpose of the universe and of all its processes and is therefore the key to their intelligibility. In this fashion, despite the extraordinary expansion of scale to a vast universe full of galaxies of stars, each with their own planetary system, and to cycles of time in which processes of formation and dissolution take place over immense periods, the history of this planet provides a key to the whole business, and this history is focussed not only in the human race, but in the present period, which will prove decisive both for the fate of this race and for the entire history of the whole universe.

We are presented with an account of a series of terrestrial stages, separated by catastrophes, going far back before the time then allowed by geologists. These stages are all populated with versions of human forms or 'races', with the later types mapped against Lyell's geological periods of the Eocene, Miocene and Pliocene (Blavatsky 1999, II: 693). By pushing the appearance of human beings back in time, she creates the possibility of her major counter to the theory of natural selection: early types of man give rise to mammalian and other vertebrate forms, explaining the appearance of gill-slits and other 'earlier' phenomena in human embryos as anticipations rather than recapitulations. And, as an instance of this reversal of the Darwinian narrative, apes are explained not as human ancestors, but as degenerate forms produced by the miscegenation of earlier races; they too are the descendants of men.

In a parallel fashion, Blavatsky reverses the contemporary assumption of progress according to which high civilization has only recently emerged from primitive conditions, and instead proposes an earlier series of civilizations with many features of our present culture, including scientific learning, which flourished and then declined, aided in their fall by periodic physical catastrophes, earthquakes and floods, to be replaced in the next cycle. In this perspective, she can account for the appearance of traces of present understandings found in ancient texts and invoke the possibility of learning passed on in secret which anticipates and reframes current advances, learning that she terms 'the Secret Doctrine'. She can also in this optic analyse the symptoms of the present age, diagnosing both its promise and the threat of decadence that its materialist doctrines indicate. The two characteristics that distinguish her occultist thought from that of 'the men of science' are, in the first place, a belief in the power of mind over matter, or intention over chance, and second, the explanation of variation in the material world through the repetitions of extensive cycles under the influence of divine minds, rather than any random accumulation of small-scale changes.

IV. The alternative path of man's development

The materials are extremely rich and the direction of the argument drawing on them is, to repeat, the reverse of that which one might naively expect. The points outlined above appear particularly clearly when Blavatsky offers what she calls the 'theosophical perspective'. Here are some illustrations, in the order she presents them, to bring out the originality of her cosmological narrative.

Before physical causes (such as selection) can operate, we have '*the physicalization of the primeval animal root-types out of the astral*' (Blavatsky

1999, II: 649), and these forms are the product of mind, an instance of the divine spirits ordering the outcome of the secondary processes.

In this (secondary) process of physical evolution, 'every living ... thing ... including man, evolved from *one common primal form*' (Blavatsky 1999, II: 659). This common derivation explains, on the one hand, the features the human embryo shares with all other animals, including recapitulation of the different forms of reproduction through which evolving life forms have passed – cellular division, hermaphroditic parthenogenesis, oviparity and sexual differentiation. On the other hand, it allows us to place the potential for memory, consciousness and speech in the prototype, a potential which may be unrealized in lower forms, or later lost.

Matching this retrospective projection of potential, Blavatsky extends human history back into the past: 'Physical man ... existed before the first bed of the Cretaceous rocks was deposited' (Blavatsky 1999, II: 679). But this early stage was not primitive; rather, 'in the early part of the Tertiary Age, the most brilliant civilization the world has ever known flourished ...' Lemuria, south of the present Continent of Asia, was the site of this earliest civilization, subsequently sinking beneath the Indian Ocean, and the form of these Lemurian men was that of 'the physical sexual creature who materialized through living aeons out of the eternal hermaphrodites' (Blavatsky 1999, II: 680). We have met some of these creatures.

Moreover, theosophical doctrine teaches that apes descended from Eocene man (Blavatsky 1999, II: 675), as a retrogressive departure from the human type (683): the apes come from the crossing of Atlantean giants of the fourth race with the degenerate products of the Lemurian third race (679; cf. 683, 688). There were, then, no apes contemporary to the origins of human civilization, and no common ancestors to be found. Blavatsky claims that this perspective resolves contemporary debates about the relation of men and gorillas and explains the lack of any intermediary remains or missing links (Blavatsky 1999, II: 681f.; see Rupke 2009 for an account of the controversies between Owen and Huxley on which she was drawing).

The production of other species from human stock is a repeated motif, for fourth round men gave rise to the mammalian fauna, while amphibians, birds, reptiles and fish arose from the same source in the third round

(Blavatsky 1999, II: 684). More primitive (invertebrate) forms, it is hinted, came from earlier (and less physical) prototypes. In short, 'all forms which now people the earth, are so many variations on *basic types* originally thrown off by the Man of the Third and Fourth Round' (Blavatsky 1999, II: 683). Returning to the earlier motif, the rudimentary organs found in embryology and employed by evolutionists may be explained instead as anticipating developments in these off-shoots of men, prototypes which 'man *shed* in the course of his astral development' (Blavatsky 1999, II: 684).

Scientific accounts ignore these earlier races and human forms, which nevertheless allow Blavatsky to integrate the archaeological discoveries of Palaeolithic and Neolithic men (Blavatsky 1999, II: 686), not to mention recently discovered hominid types such as *Dryopithecus*. To preserve the ape-theory, scientists must confine man's origins to the late Tertiary period (Blavatsky 1999, II: 687f.).

Everything hangs, then, on the antiquity of human forms. Blavatsky plays on uncertainties in contemporary estimates concerning the age of the earth, the period of animal evolution, and the place of man in these accounts (Blavatsky 1999, II: 694–699). In the last case, she points to acknowledged problems with the theory of selection, particularly the time required, to Huxley's recourse to 'saltations' or jumps in evolution to explain gaps in the fossil record, and to the lack of evidence for transitional forms. Her focus is on the insufficiency of an accumulation of small, random changes to account both for the long-established variety of distinct forms found in the fossil deposits and with the sudden emergence of new types of bodily organization. She instead invokes external causes and brings in an entire apparatus organized by external minds: the antiquity of the planetary chain, seven rounds of planetary life, the separation of the human races into seven Root Races, the antiquity even of modern man (found in this fourth round), and the changing form of organic life with every Root-Race, altering from ethereality to materiality and back (Blavatsky 1999, II: 697). This apparatus brings us – finally – to a plurality of inhabited worlds.

This framing allows her to combine data from the sciences and from occultism, mapping the classification of geological strata by the fossil record they contain on to a schema which she claims to have derived from a synthesis of the wisdom of ancient civilizations (Blavatsky 1999, II: 710–713). She can then suggest that Primordial, Secondary and Tertiary rocks all contain evidence pointing to the existence of the third (Lemurian) race, together with relics of earlier periods. Human history is made contemporary with the age of reptiles and the appearance of now-extinct mammals. And evidence is presented, too, that man as we know him now, the fourth race, begins with the civilization of Atlantis.

This long human history is organized around two themes. First, there is a progressive force at work that organizes matter, both inorganic and organic, which is born witness to by evidence of early sophistication. And second, there is a corresponding notion of decline and the falling-away of higher types, a theme which is accompanied by that of periodic physical catastrophes, with the raising of mountains and inundations of land masses. The last chapters are concerned with progress in the natural world, in the forms of speciation and the origins of the larger divisions in the plant and animal kingdoms (Blavatsky 1999, II: 735–736), and with equivalent evidences of vitality in earlier civilizations, such as rumours of giants in the submerged continent of Atlantis. Blavatsky can suggest that memories of these past places, creatures and events are contained in traditional wisdom and folklore and can link together talk of Atlanteans and Lemurians, rumours of dwarfish races and Titans, with speculation on antiquities such as dolmens and past 'Cyclopean' civilizations (presumably based on the Easter Island statues), to which she attributes colossal buildings (see Blavatsky 1999, II: 749, 754, 755, 775, 752, 769).

These fragments of ancient wisdom – records, not myths nor revelation, she says – overturn the claims to originality of both modern science and theology, and establish a source to be drawn on, traces of which can be discovered both in the scriptures of the various religions and in the writings of earlier occultists (Blavatsky 1999, II: 794ff.). She makes the problem of the depth of geological time central to the right interpretation of the evidence, and the solution lies in Blavatsky's offering, 'The Secret Doctrine', 'the key of Wisdom [which] can unlock the religion of Nature' (Blavatsky 1999, II: 797).

The planetary system mapped

Modern scientific discoveries can in this way be put to cosmological purposes, defining man's place in the expanded Universe. What can be learnt from this account of the development of human life in the context of the history of the planets, if we focus on our interest in the history of science fiction? What are the broad lines of the narrative that emerges?

First, the evolution of man, in the sense of his moral progress, involves a planetary system, and does not take place on earth alone. And progressive evolution demands successive lives lived in different spheres and some account of the transmission of merit (evaluative memory) to match up to the scale of the setting.

Second, spirit monads travel between planets, spending long periods on each as they develop.

Third, there are corresponding states of planets and spirit monads, as both cycle between ethereal and material forms, descending into material life and ascending out of it.

Fourth, spirits, matching their environing planets, exist in more material and more ethereal forms. The more ethereal forms are invisible to the more material but not vice versa, and, on the upward branch of ascent, will possess more advanced mental powers that will allow them to monitor, understand and communicate with the less advanced forms. In this fashion, advanced spirits may come to the assistance of more backward forms and even help them to progress to another stage.

Fifth, the Earth as we know it, found at the most material stage of the cycle, is crucial from the perspective of moral progress, for although here the spiritual elements are balanced and limited by the material, it is only in this material incarnation that the fate of the soul can be worked out and the upward path gained. The entire system turns around the present Earth, conceived as a moment of crisis (in the sense of judgement). And the secret teachings of Theosophy which allow an understanding of this moment and the possibility of grasping the opportunity it offers therefore have an extraordinary significance, for the individual, for the race, and for the system as a whole. This is the structure of occult knowledge: a secret, an individual vocation or calling, an organization in which to pursue it, and a chance to participate in the salvation of humankind and, through it, the fate of the Universe.

In sum, we find a planetary system populated by intentional life forms, some of which are gifted with advanced mental powers and scientific understanding, focussed on a moment of crisis in earthly affairs. All this is set in the perspective of man's progressive evolution, and through periodic encounters with more advanced forms, we gain glimpses of an organizing principle, a World Soul or Cosmic Mind. Finally, those on earth who hold advanced understanding, either from scientific or occult sources, possess the keys to the system and are the best guarantors of the progress of the human race past this eschatological horizon and on to salvation. In this fashion, all the elements of the science fiction genre we have identified had been placed within a single structure by the 1880s.

We can make three further observations pertinent to the future of science fiction as a style of thought. The first is that Blavatsky's teleological argument is marked by a shift from a concept of time as chronology – a sequence of before and after along an objective scale – to one of synchronicities and duration. A scientific account tends to treat time simply as a neutral milieu for events and processes; a teleological account sees time as recursive and active, producing anticipations and repetitions. To make the distinction, we might note that time travel is a nonsense only in a world of neutral time; once intentionality is introduced as a world-condition, clairvoyance, being in advance of one's time, helping lead less advanced persons forward and aiding progress, all become possible. This temporal aspect may be a feature of rival models of how language works ('language ideologies' – see Jenkins 2013). These rival forms can interact; the question is, which ideology predominates, and under what circumstances? Time in the teleological sense becomes a matter of performance, when people construct synchronicities and duration and so make events happen. Timing becomes everything; fitness, reputation and status are crucial to achieving some end, as is controlling multiple variants, and timing of this kind, we might suppose, is only possible when the underlying frame of reference is shifting. In other words, teleological systems emerge with force precisely under conditions of what Ardener (2007) calls 'parameter collapse'.

There is a further observation at issue here, which applies more generally to the science fiction genre. Blavatsky takes these points of disturbance which she has identified, the overturning of certainties and the multiplication of possibilities, and, instead of exploiting their disruptive potential, she puts them to a conservative end. She uses them to construct an argument against multiplicity and contingency and in favour of a universe which, although vast and endlessly complex, is organized in every part by intentional action, working according to a few constant ordering principles, with a benign purpose for both individuals and mankind as a race at their heart. We may experience crisis, but the point is to overcome the crisis and to re-join the progressive story which is being told. The theodicy illustrates what Wittenberg refers to as the 'law of the Conservation of Reality' (2013: 151): all this radical work is done to restore a recognizable universe, one which has the well-being of humanity at its core. Despite its exotic guise, this approach bears the marks of a distinctively liberal Protestant mind-set.

And third, relating to both these observations, Theosophy develops a series of linked concepts relating to memory, its preservation and recovery, which also appear in science fiction stories. In principle, the past is recorded in its totality and can be restored; there is a complete memory of the processes, which is termed the 'Akashic record'. This operates at every scale. The Secret Doctrine is a summary of its recensions. Further, there is a set of people who have access to this record; this is the college or lodge of Masters, who not only can resort to hidden libraries where this material is accumulated but also have direct access by intuition or a sixth sense. The self-narrative of Theosophy turns around recovering this total memory, appropriate to the period of invention of the possibility of total recording, storage and transmission of information. Moreover, this memory is not simply the living record of the natural processes of cosmological evolution, nor just the history of the races and their civilizations, discoveries and wisdom; it is both those things, but also operates at the personal level, in terms of being able to recall past lives, in different stages of development. These memories are also part of the Akashic record. This memory can be reached by training and dedication; access is the result of discipline in the hands of special teachers with remarkable gifts. When achieved and uncovered, it is literally true, and it relates to every level of the past, every scale of activity, from the cosmic to the microscopic or even atomic. This complex of ideas about memory reappears in various guises.

Other planets, other life-forms

The Secret Doctrine is organized on a grand scale, beginning from the self-differentiating productions of the Universal Mind and elaborated through a succession of 'vehicles' – gods, planetary spirits, Adepts and so forth – guiding every level of activity in the universe. As I have suggested, the notion of spirit beings found on other planets is not the focus of the argument, and yet references to such beings recur throughout the two books. I will give examples taken mostly from the appendices where Blavatsky reviews contemporary scientific materials and in which she refines her constructive images and metaphors.

In a discussion of the metaphysical nature of the 'elements and atoms' (Blavatsky 1999, I: 566–578), Blavatsky takes up contemporary notions of atoms as the elementary units but claims, in a fashion we now recognize, that modern science restricts itself to considering the chains of cause and effect in which they participate. The scientific approach thereby neglects both the question of the origin of the energy at work in such chains of repeated mechanical causes and effects and that of what motivates simple elements to take part in higher forms of complex organization. Modern science, she suggests, engages in an infinite regress, on the one hand, and has no explanation of pattern or order, on the other.

She answers these challenges in general terms by proposing a sequence of transformations that runs from the Universal Mind to the simple atom or monad, according to three principles: a sequence of emanations, by which the Cosmic Mind differentiates itself into a series of levels; a cycle of descent from spirit into matter, followed by ascent again to the spiritual; and 'Karmic law', through which repeated cycles allow the expression of the unity of the whole system (Blavatsky 1999, I: 14–17). If we begin the cycle from the Universal Spirit, it emanates seven 'incorporeal beings', which in turn create 'celestial selves'. Blavatsky calls these prototypes, which appear as stars, the 'seven sons of light', each presiding over one of the seven planets, 'the spheres of the indwelling seven spirits', being the principle through which each human group is formed and guided. These planetary spirits are called after their planets, namely, 'Saturn, Jupiter, Mercury, Mars, Venus and ... the Sun and Moon'; the other planets – Uranus and Neptune – are, we are told, involved in 'other septenary chains of globes in our system' (Blavatsky 1999, I: 575).

These celestial selves, besides being the ordering principles of the planets and founding each cycle through a series of further emanations, descending into material form and rising out of it, may also appear in human form (in our world), 'born ... (on earth) again and again' (Blavatsky 1999, I: 571), acting as guides, spirits in human form instructing and elevating humans. Blavatsky gives these spirits the name 'Dhyan Chohans'; they appear as spiritual leaders such as the Buddha, but also as Adepts, each though material participating in higher mental forms.

Given that everything is animated by participation in spirit or mind, and that life passes from planet to planet in a series of progressions, a repeated motif is the improvement of human culture by intelligent creatures from other planets. A typical passage describes the role of the Moon (and other 'planets') in the construction of the Earth's life, drawing in this instance from Jewish sources:

> Lunar magnetism generates life, preserves and destroys it, psychically as well as physically. But if, astronomically, she is one of the seven planets of the ancient world, in theogony she is one of the regents thereof ... The worshippers of the *Teraphim* (the Jewish Oracles) "carved images and claimed that the light of the principal stars (planets) permeating these through and through, the angelic VIRTUES (or the regents of the stars and planets) conversed with them, teaching them many most useful things and arts". And Seldenus explains that the *Teraphim* were built and composed after the position of certain planets ... and called ... the *tutelary* gods .... (Blavatsky 1999, I: 394)

These lunar spirits taught men their skill, permitted divination, and helped the construction of the Temple; all this is testified to in ancient traditions of lunar worship, Blavatsky claims. She traces a brief history of this religion, beginning with the third race of our round, becoming a power of sorcery to the fourth race, the Atlanteans, and leading in the fifth race to division and conflict between male and female cults, devoted to solar and lunar gods respectively (Blavatsky 1999, I: 397).

This brief excursus gives some sense of Blavatsky's style, with its eclecticism and power of synthesis; she explains these characteristics as an expression of the principle that intelligence or spirit acts at every level of the universe; the occultist, she says, is concerned with 'the Soul and Spirit of Cosmic Space' (Blavatsky 1999, I: 589), and not simply with appearances and behaviour, looking to such questions as 'whence matter itself; whence the evolutionary impetus determining its cyclic aggregations and dissolutions; whence the exquisite symmetry and order into which the primeval atoms arrange and group themselves?' (Blavatsky 1999, I: 591–592). The ordering forms of material existence are attributed to disembodied intelligences, to planetary spirits and their avatars.

This focus on intelligent life elsewhere and the properties of mind not only allows the reinterpretation of ancient religious texts but also the intuition of physical laws. To take a single instance, paralleling the properties attributed to the Moon, Blavatsky relates the distribution of the physical life-giving principle, 'Vital Electricity', to proximity to the Sun, concluding 'therefore, the men on Mars are more ethereal than we are, while those on Venus are more gross, though far more intelligent, if less spiritual' (Blavatsky 1999, I: 602). The phenomena of cause and effect are controlled at every scale by the rule of analogy.

Blavatsky not only defends the reality of conscious life elsewhere and the plurality of inhabitable other worlds, populated by other forms of life, but also appeals to other, invisible worlds to be found here on Earth. She lists 'Sylphs, Salamanders, Undines, and Gnomes' (Blavatsky 1999, I: 606), detectable only by a further, psychic, sense, invoking the analogy of microscopic life forms, present but invisible to the naked eye (Blavatsky 1999, I: 608f.). Furthermore, she links this claim of lower spirit forms to her initial insight into the multiple orders of life in a teeming Universe: 'Kosmos, besides its objective planetary inhabitants, its humanities in other inhabited worlds, is full of invisible, intelligent *Existences*', naming 'Arch-Angels, Angels and Spirits of the West … the Dhyan-Chohans, the Devas and Pitris, of the East' (Blavatsky 1999, I: 611).

Book II is organized, as we have seen, around the proposition that men did not descend from the apes but, on the contrary, were formed earlier than apes, with the corollary that the fossil apes recently discovered arose from the crossing of Atlantean giants with the remnants of Lemurians, that is, from miscegenation between earlier races of men. The question then arises, where did men come from? The Theosophical account is that man 'shows his origins from a type far superior to himself. And this type is the "Heavenly man" – the Dhyan Chohans or the *Pitris* so-called' (Blavatsky 1999, II: 683). This hint is taken up a few pages later in a discussion of the possible plurality of inhabited worlds. Blavatsky asks: 'How do we know (a) what kind of Beings inhabit the globes [planets] in general; and (b) whether *those* who rule planets superior to our own, do not exercise the same influence on our earth *consciously*, that we may exercise *unconsciously* – say on the small planets (planetoids or asteroids) in the long run, by our cutting the Earth to pieces, opening canals, and thereby entirely changing our climates' (Blavatsky 1999, II: 700).

She is clear that we cannot know anything of matters beyond our solar system, criticizing 'the romances as in all so-called scientific fictions and spiritistic *revelations* from moons, stars, and planets' (Blavatsky 1999, II: 701), fictions which do no more than recombine elements drawn from the life we know here. She includes Swedenborg, normally beyond reproach, in this complaint. We must confine our reasoning to this planetary system; even Adepts, who can enter into mental rapport with other planes of consciousness present in this system and thereby gain experiences which cannot readily be communicated to the ordinary mind, cannot go further.

Nonetheless, because of the rule of analogy, she can assert that 'most of the planets, as the stars beyond our system, are inhabited', citing Flammarion among others on the conditions for life elsewhere and concluding that 'Life – intelligent, conscious life – *must* exist on other worlds than ours' (Blavatsky 1999, II: 702). She can therefore place Earth in the context of five hundred million stars (Blavatsky 1999, II: 708) but confines her more detailed speculations as to the appropriate conditions for the development of life and intelligence, and of resident populations, on the neighbouring planets of Jupiter, Venus, Mercury and Mars (Blavatsky 1999, II: 707).

Returning to the question of human origins, we have repeated mention of the formative influences that shape humankind coming from outside the Earth, as in this instance: 'it is the "Soul", or the *inner* man, that descends on Earth first, the psychic *astral*, the mould on which physical man is gradually built – his Spirit, intellectual and moral faculties awakening later on as that physical stature grows and develops' (Blavatsky 1999, II: 728). We glimpse a process rather than a single moment, a series of interventions by intentional spirit minds coming from other planets, all the time acting through natural means, through which man is first formed physically and then developed spiritually. Blavatsky can trace the gradual materialization and refinement of the human form through the earlier races, noting, incidentally, that the 'evolution of *physiological* Man out of the astral races of *early* Lemurian age – the Jurassic age of Geology – is exactly paralleled by the "materialization" of "spirits" ... in the séance room ...' (Blavatsky 1999, II: 737).

In like fashion, Blavatsky explains the issues of speciation and of the origins of the higher divisions of the animal kingdom by the actions of presiding spirits and the astral prototypes passing into physical forms (Blavatsky 1999, II: 735–736). In sum, the action of planetary spirits is the element needed to explain the direction of evolution and the nature of the forms adopted.

These actors return at intervals throughout the entire length of *The Secret Doctrine*, because its purpose is to describe the descent of man starting from the origins of the Cosmos, passing through the formation of the Universe and the planets, encompassing the emergence of life and coming to a focus in the present call to mankind to return to unity with the Universal Mind which lies behind the entire process. They are the ghosts in the machine, responsible for form and purpose at every level.

These processes are capable of infinite refinement in Blavatsky's hands, refinements which constitute both the reward and the difficulty of reading the text. As a last small example of elaboration, the 'Sons of Fire ... the deities which preside over the Cosmo-psychic Powers' (Blavatsky 1999, I: 86) can be divided into lunar deities who created physical man, and solar deities, who fashion the Inner Man. This division of lunar and solar powers also corresponds to that between purification of the senses on the one hand

and of mental illusions on the other (Blavatsky 1999, I: 87; cf. 180–182). This elaborative approach of Blavatsky's may be thought of as anti-Occam's razor: we add in extra levels of explanation beyond the known/material, organized not by empiricism but by the number seven, and taught to the elect by hidden Masters, according to the period of development of the Cosmic Mind. In a sociological perspective, we might wonder whether only small, coherent groups can afford such agreed, arbitrary elaborations (although all collective representations have powers of freezing the frame and developing independent elaborations – see Jenkins 1994: 438); perhaps larger, more diffuse societies can only work by conventions such as materialist reductions: coarse, inaccurate, but functional at a certain scale.

At the same time, there is a simple, ordering thread linking spirit controls, planetary beings and Adepts here on Earth; each is a version of the others, capable of guiding us through the tangle of detail that constitutes knowledge of the world and the universe, a secret learning given form in Theosophy's doctrines.

We shall now return to Shaver's version of this ordered universe.

CHAPTER 3

The 'Shaver Mystery' – sources and commentary

Blavatsky's inclusion of practically every facet of contemporary scholarship and scientific research was made possible by invoking a hierarchy of spirits, who in return are stretched by this learning's new dimensions: they become intentional, mindful beings who organize both physical energies and the evolution of man, creating Nature and human history at every stage and scale, and they integrate both natural and moral law. In this fashion, we discover not only other possible forms of life, capable of raising civilizations and advanced technologies on other planets, but also, that these planetary beings are intimately concerned with life on Earth and with human development, which they monitor and regulate by using advanced mental powers, being able to read human minds, foresee the consequences of human actions, and communicate with chosen individuals by such means as telepathy.

I. Sources and dissemination

It would be another kind of work to trace the uptake of this complex of ideas and its being put to work in early science fiction. I am not suggesting that Blavatsky's work is the sole parent of the genre; far from it. There were various elements widely present, among them a fascination with the promise of new technologies, speculation about the implications of the expansion of the dimensions of time and space (as well as the possibilities of time travel and the 'fourth dimension' in overcoming these expansions), and attempts to seize on and use the implications of the latest scientific discoveries concerning both the nature of matter and the nature of mind, including the early findings of psychological science prompted by psychical research. And these were taken up in many combinations by a range of popular writers; science fiction emerged as a minor strand among types of pulp fiction, and had a variety of guises, including encouraging the technical amateur, what became known as 'space opera', and (slightly later) a strand of imaginative reflection on the implications of the present condition of things (see Ashley and Lowndes 2004). But the synthesis of elements offered by the theosophists was both complete, in terms of including all the relevant elements, and peculiarly appropriate, because it offered a moral narrative or theodicy, with its implications of scale, threat, critique, and eventual outcome. This synthesis can be tracked in the early pulp literature in both borrowings of plot elements and terminology, but by the 'Golden Age' (1940s–1960s), this narrative structure has become the predominant 'grammar' of the genre, with a human-focussed universe and extraordinary mental powers the stuff of many classics, even though the borrowings of vocabulary in large part fall away. This grammar continues to structure a good deal of writing to the present day, including those authors exploring the contemporary themes of Artificial Intelligence and the Singularity.

Shaver's work exhibits both the borrowing of vocabulary and the adoption of the ground-rules. We might notice the circle that runs from the wise instructors who mentor the apprentices, the physics that passes from particles to planetary systems, the accompanying technologies, the cycles of life at every scale and the mental properties that characterize each level, and the idea of an accessible memory of the whole process, a record which can be recovered, taught and set to work in each new circumstance.

There is one further factor to be mentioned in sketching the realization of the theosophical dream in popular literature. Blavatsky's writings are complex, stimulating and mysterious, and they lack any clear structure or easily grasped argument. Blavatsky's ideas, however, have been disseminated in large part through the writings of C. W. Leadbeater (1847–1934). Blavatsky's role in the Theosophical Society was taken over at her death in 1891 by Annie Besant (1847–1933), who combined intellectual and organizational skills of a high order (see Nethercot 1960, 1963), but Besant relied a good deal for guidance on Leadbeater, who had had but a marginal role in Theosophy during Blavatsky's lifetime. Where Blavatsky built up ambiguities and levels of interpretation, Leadbeater produced writings notable for their 'apparent factual simplicity' (Tillett 1982: 260), writing on every occult topic in a clear and accessible style. Tillett's biography lists these topics: 'Masters, reincarnation, karma, Akashic records, Atlantis, Lemuria, Shamballa, astral plane, Monad, vibrations and psychic powers' (Tillett 1982: 261); he could have added chakras, clairvoyance, dreams, occult chemistry, auras, the heavenly world, the fourth dimension, invisible helpers, previous lives, and far, far more.[1] In every case, Leadbeater offered a detailed classification of the topic under consideration, ordering materials and making distinctions. His technique was to work by clairvoyance, receiving direct inspiration from his teachers and transcribing the knowledge of other worlds that he received in this fashion, often in the form of dramatic histories or narratives of past lives. Just as he simplified and instrumentalized Blavatsky's techniques, so he operationalized her concepts, for example, dwelling a good deal on the reality of dark forces opposing his advice and policies. While, as Tillett notes, his simplifications often contrast with the sophistication of Blavatsky's teachings, for this reason they have been influential in occult writings of many kinds, and Leadbeater's work rather than Blavatsky's has been the source of much of the transfer of theosophical ideas. It would be a further labour to trace the precise source of each writers' borrowings, whether, for example, Shaver's account of the history of Atlantis came directly from Blavatsky (1888) or was mediated through Sinnett (1883), Scott Elliot (1896) or Besant and Leadbeater (1913).

In short, it is through Theosophy that spirits occupy our skies, fly between planets, concern themselves with human lives and shape our history. If they let themselves be seen, it is because their intention is that we should come to be like them, overcoming the limits of materiality and learning to share their mental powers, and in this fashion returning to participate in the Cosmic Mind. They – the spirits – serve as the means of seizing opportunities created by shifts in the categories by which we grasp the nature of

---

1   I have looked at *The Astral Plane* (1895), *Man Visible and Invisible* (1902), *Man: Whence, How and Whither* (1913, co-authored with Besant), and *The Masters and The Path* (1925).

the real, shifts that are the effects of scientific discoveries and advances in technology, opportunities that are realized in new moral practices.

While we have now surveyed the ground rules organizing Shaver's story, two contemporary features stand out. The first is a complex theory of vitalism 'explaining' the differences between the distinct races of Titans and Nortans, humans (culture men) and abandondero. The second is the enthusiasm with which he adopts new scientific and technological discoveries and produces innovations on these themes within the overall moral narrative of call, struggle and progress. They play different roles, the first allowing the transfer of racial theories to later materials, the other an index of the ability of theosophical ideas to accommodate new scientific ideas and debates. We shall look at each in turn, before discussing how this theosophical inheritance was put to work in its contemporary American context.

Sources for racial differences

Christopher Roth (2005) focusses on the sources of the theme of racial diversity in Shaver and more broadly in American Metaphysical groups, the UFO movement in particular. He makes two points. The first is that American discussions of life on other planets draw on earlier schemes that derive from 'paradigms in physical anthropology', so prolonging a 'hierarchical racial and class order' (Roth 2005: 41), and that these schemes, whilst emerging in a zone between the nascent human sciences and less official discourses (in the late nineteenth and early twentieth centuries) and promoted in the esoteric circles from which the first flying saucer reports were made after 1945, also persist in more subtle forms in the scientific discussions of alien life that develop from the 1960s (Roth 2005: 42–43). In short, 'terrestrial racial schemes' deriving from early anthropological discussions persist in a variety of contemporary debates, in such areas as both scientific creationism and ufology.

Roth's second point is, as we might expect, that these 'esoteric anthropologies' were transmitted above all through the influence of Theosophy, expressed in certain 'vigorous continuities in ideology, worldview, and language' (Roth 2005: 43) among a range of organizations and authors. Theosophy helped create a 'vernacular anthropology' which stands as a distinct cultural resource in twentieth-century discussions of other forms of intentional life. Albanese (2007: 498–501) makes much the same point. Blavatsky's work is clearly central to understanding the racial scheme, the vocabulary and the vitalism which helps structure Shaver's account, and which also contributes to the ideas of other early figures in the flying saucer movement such as George Adamski and George Hunt Williamson (see Roth 2005: 47–58). The cosmology developed by the medium Mrs. Keech in the early 1950s also owes many of its ideas to this occult source (see Festinger et al. 1956, cf. Jenkins 2013: 27–31).

Roth notes how Blavatsky offers a progressive, though interrupted, evolutionary narrative distinct from Darwin's theory, one which distributes a range of actors over a period extending far beyond a standard human history of the period and beyond the earth. Here we find a good many of the elements Shaver employs: Lemurians and Atlanteans as predecessors to the human race (Titans also appear in a minor role, as the memories of giants), the sexual energy of the Lemurians, the sense of a decline in vitality and wisdom from the original great souls or Ancient Masters, and the countervailing sense of progressive evolution towards a Coming Race, with both the calling that potential creates and also a realization of the immense obstacles that stand in its way.

Roth also draws attention to other elements of this improvisation. There are interplanetary ideas: the original Root-Race arrived from the moon, and the Lemurians were taught agriculture, weaving and other technologies by the inhabitants of Venus, who are far in advance of earthly civilizations. The Venusians also established secret societies – the occult lodges of the Masons and the Rosicrucians, anticipating the role of the theosophical lodges – to pass on wisdom to later societies. The fifth Root-Race are named as the Aryans, drawing on Max Müller's 'classification of language stocks as a method for sorting out the genealogy of races ... [and] privileging the revealed religions of India, not Judeo-Christian ones, as the original connection with the divine'. The role of the Anglo-Saxons, an Aryan sub-race, was to come to prominence in the present period as part of a divinely ordained sequence (see Roth 2005: 47).

The overall message concerns, first, the emergence of a new Root-Race with secret knowledge of their position in the whole process, knowledge embodied in the Theosophists, together with, second, an understanding of the various contingent agencies of change – eugenic engineering, extraterrestrial intervention, continental sinkings and climate change – which accompany this central process, and, third, a call to join this elect group and to share in the transmission of its vital message to the world, a message both of judgement and of hope. It is an extraordinary autodidact anticipation of modernist thought in its outline, offering a new voice describing an unprecedented world condition with novel natural, scientific and social features; it had many offspring in the 1920s and later, including Lovecraft and Shaver, both of whom tended to put a pessimistic spin on things. Roth indeed sees Palmer and Shaver as using Blavatsky in 'setting the scene', offering a 'coherent occult schema' (Roth 2005: 48) which the first contactees, Adamski and Williamson, could employ to produce the scenarios of flying saucer reports, through which this racially inflected ideology is transmitted.

A further remark: Shaver's racial scheme also maps distributions of social class differences. The Titan elite combines aristocracy, education, wealth and political power in a virtual monopoly, while in principle benignly looking after the interests and training of the 'mediocro' or middle class. And the abandondero class represent a proletariat, working underground, as in Lang's *Metropolis* (1927). Indeed, we have a social picture that repeats features of Wells' vision of a decadent ruling class, the Eloi, threatened by the technocratic subterranean Morlocks, who feed on their former masters (see *The Time Machine: An Invention*', 1895). Yet, while Shaver appears to expect the restoration of racial and social harmony as a result of the return to a reconciled, rightly ordered world, he seeks no systematic reform and so, in practice, anticipates a different future in which social and racial conflict and exploitation will be a permanent theme. This is part of the inheritance he leaves.

Shaver's engagement with contemporary scientific discoveries

Although Roth legitimately focusses on the continuity of racial ideas and their transference to 1940s America, the theosophical contribution to Shaver's thought can also equally be traced in his engagement with contemporary scientific debates. Toronto has identified some of his scientific sources, drawing on his correspondence and unpublished notes (see Toronto 2013: 106ff.). A principal influence was Albert Crehore, an inventor with patents in telegraphy, electromagnetism and the measurement of high-speed projectiles, and writer on the fundamental forces in physics. Crehore published an early article, 'Analysis of the Causes of Gravitation' (1912) and a series of books beginning with *The Atom* in 1920. Shaver improvised on these theories in his account of exd, a fine ash permeating the Universe which is attracted to large planetary bodies, which by that means accumulate. 'The friction that exd creates in the processes of being absorbed into planetary bodies is what we experience as gravity' (Toronto 2013: 107). The integrative force of exd is matched by a counter, disintegrative force; they together appear in Shaver's Gnostic worldview as good and bad rays respectively, controlled by distinct species ('teros' and 'deros'). In a footnote in 'I Remember Lemuria', Shaver also discusses the possibility of powering space flight by an antigravitational device which eliminates the frictional effects of exd. In this instance, pulp science fiction plays on part of the field of contemporary physics, one that rejects the innovations of Quantum Theory being developed and its simplifications. While Crehore's explanations have now been set aside, they were not eccentric in the period, and they provide underlying forms of coherence that permitted the narrative to develop.[2]

Crehore also had interests in the prevention of aging, and in correspondence pointed Shaver to the works of Raymond Pearl and George Crile.

---

[2] It is hard to know whether to read significance into Shaver's preference for an eventual loser – a discarded hypothesis – in the competition with Quantum Theory. It may well be that he found integrative elements in Crehore's account which suited his teleological narrative, elements which, in the longer term, disqualified the account.

Pearl was the author of the *Biology of Death* (1920). Crile, a distinguished surgeon, published *The Phenomenon of Life. A Radio Electric Interpretation* (1936), in which he outlined a theory of the life force which, he suggested, resulted from the work of the endocrine system, the brain and the sympathetic nervous system together processing radiant energy from the sun and cosmos, converting it into a shortwave electromagnetic field. At the same time, he identified points in the protoplasm of cells – 'radiogens' – that could emit intense rays of this life force. Like Crehore's theory of gravity, these vitalist themes have not gained wide consent in the scientific community over time, but they allow the integration of extensive physical forces with questions of individual aging, disease and death, which Shaver could employ in his theodicy. At the least, their use indicates Shaver's detailed engagement with the developing sciences of his time, updating the frame taken from Theosophy.

I want now to draw out the form this schema took in Shaver and the contemporary elements he made sense of through it; in short, we want to see how this theosophical approach was put to work in the 1940s.

Collective development of the saga

The 'Shaver mystery', as Palmer called it, was expanded through a series of further articles, published and re-published by him as editor. Here is Kripal, reflecting on Ray Palmer's part in Shaver's larger account:

> According to Palmer's reconstruction ... [Shaver's] original story was about how the earth's earliest inhabitants fled the surface when the sun's radiation became too extreme about twelve thousand years ago. The lucky ones, the immortal ones called Titans or Atlans, fled their underground civilization and left in spaceships. They now live in the blackness of outer space, where they need no longer fear a star's radiation. The not so lucky ones, the abandoned ones (called abandonderos), fled into the bowels of the earth, where they developed into two distinct races: the insane and largely sinister deros (for "detrimental robots") and the good and noble teros (for "integrative robots"). Alas, the former soon outnumbered the latter and have been haunting and using the abandoned technology of the Titans and Atlans to zap the poor fools who could not escape into space or the underworld ever since – that is, us. We don't remember any of this any longer ... All we have left are vague folk memories

of "Atlantis" and "Lemuria" and weird stories about various species of giants, ogres, little people, gremlins, and devils which, according to Shaver, are really all deros ... that, or false projections beamed up by the deros. (Kripal 2011: 99–100)[3]

Kripal brings out Shaver's interest in sexual energies as well as his striking pessimism: a 'worldview ... in which pretty much everything of importance was traced back to evil deros and sinister machines in the hollow earth' (Kripal 2011: 101). The unseen world beneath us is 'complete in its mastery of Earth' (Shaver, quoted in Wentworth 1973), and notions of 'God, an afterlife, a spiritual world, or paranormal powers' (Kripal 2011: 103) are all the illusory effects of ray machines. In effect, any complex human experience is artificially produced; as Kripal comments, Shaver was an extreme materialist, without any notion of projection or capacity to think in terms of symbols or metaphors.

Roth gives a parallel account of the saga, again presenting a broader synthesis from the dialectic of readers' responses and subsequent stories:

> Shaver asserted that Earth was first peopled by a race of extraterrestrial Titans. Making their home on Atlantis, they created "robot races" to serve them, but an increasing bombardment of lethal solar rays, which truncated the Titans' originally Methuselah-like life spans, drove them to build and inhabit a network of caves, which honeycomb the Earth today. Failing to escape the solar rays even there, the Titans migrated to another star, but there was not enough room on their rockets for all the robot races, who were left behind. Some of these returned to the surface as they adapted to the changed atmosphere; these are humanity's ancestors. Others stayed underground; they survive today in two groups: the Deros, who de-evolved into a race of evil "midget-like idiots", and a smaller population of Teros who continue to resist them. Most wars, plagues, and other ills are caused by Deros wielding the machines abandoned by the Titans, which fire fiendish "stim" rays. These stim rays are also used to broadcast voices into surface-dwellers' heads – which is how Shaver learned of this complex history. (Roth 2005: 49)[4]

---

3   Kripal's sources are Palmer (1975) – the first volume of a projected autobiography – together with *The Forum*, a series of fans' letters and Palmer's replies, and Wentworth (1973).

4   Roth draws on Palmer (1975), Kafton-Minkel (1989) and Keel (1986).

In the next section, I want to draw out three sociological features which, although present, tend to be underplayed in these and other discussions of Shaver. These are, first, the theme of time travel and the narrative frame it permits, bringing past and present into contact; second, the play in the account between unifying principles of explanation and dispersive forces, representing teleological and contingent tendencies respectively; and third, the significance of new media in the characterization of the modern world, which is structured by the transmission and storage of information, threatened by the breakdown of communication (or its misuse) and motivated by the desire for direct, mind-to-mind, contact (which translate respectively these dispersive and unifying forces). The last is the most extensive discussion. In this fashion, we can see how theosophical ideas were realized in pulp fiction and, contrariwise, how they helped to interpret contemporary experiences. They prepare the way for later readings.

II. Commentary

Time travel

If we follow Wittenberg (2013), some of the effects of modern physics (space-time curvature, inter-dimensionality, and temporal relativity) are found in science fiction, which can be taken as a 'literature about encountering (or reencountering) oneself, about meeting (or remeeting) one's progenitors, about negotiating (or renegotiating) one's personal and historical origins' (Wittenberg 2013: 64). This writing concerns such themes as coming to know the self, understanding the past in a new light, and constructing new possibilities for the future on these new grounds (all versions of a Protestant vocation; cf. William James 1902). The feature of recovering the past is crucial for theosophical ideas, for the Secret Doctrine is an exact record of past insights captured at specific historical moments – called the 'Akashic record' – to the extent that becoming a theosophist is learning to participate in this literal memory. Recovering such an authentic but obscured memory is a continuing theme in the materials we shall examine.

These claims of reencounter are borne out by Shaver's story, where a narrative about the planet's past gives us a key to understanding our present situation. Moreover, Wittenberg is supported in his further claim that the basic scheme of such narratives is visual in nature – a 'literal depiction of the ... conditions under which viewpoint is constructed' (Wittenberg 2013: 147). 'Space Opera' as a genre was made possible by film as much as radio, exploiting the filmic and radiophonic property of manipulating the time axis. We have already mentioned the parallel between Shaver and film noir, particularly in the flashbacks needed to decipher the present and create retrospectively alternative understandings that unmask the truth behind surface appearances.

Wittenberg appears to be right, too, in his further suggestion that, although psychoanalytic potentials of an oedipal and narcissistic kind are clearly present in the business of going back in time and meeting one's ancestors, these possibilities are largely ignored in the genre we are concerned with, and that instead the narrative adheres to a basic conservatism, which we have already met as the 'law of the Conservation of Reality'. Although we are introduced to the most appalling disruptive forces (the malicious rays of the deros), we meet them at the point of crisis, when they are overcome by a combination of individual initiative (by Mutan and his companions) and the aid of a god-in-the-machine (the incorruptible and quasi-omnipotent Vanue).

Time travel presents a series of paradoxes around the question of knowledge: if you travel to the past (or the future), surely you will simply be an actor in that other world, just as at present you are simply an actor in this world, without any sense of comparison between times. Yet the purpose of this kind of story is to draw in the reader to another time, extending the call from the narrator to the reader to restore the natural order against a threat which has its roots in the past.

The prime device which allows the correction of past deviations is the creation within the text of a figure who can represent the reader and see both times, uncovering the causes of the situation and hence revealing the alternative courses possible. In this fashion, a persistent memory of the genealogy of the narrative is created that functions both within and beyond the story, so that all the actors live within the story, except the hero who discovers the back-story and conveys it to the reader. In Mutan's case, he is given the specific task of making a record for future man, so that he and the reader are both within and outside the story. He exhibits what we may (following Wittenberg) call 'narratological clairvoyance', which allows him, by manipulations along the time axis, to reunite the forces of dispersion into a single tale, and so to restore the conditions of ordinary life. The recovered memories of abductees play a similar function.

It is worth drawing attention to the parallels with a better-known, contemporary account, George Orwell's *Nineteen Eighty-Four*, published in 1949. Orwell likewise was concerned with manipulations of appearances by hidden centralized authorities, through devices such as 'Newspeak' and 'double think', and with the associated puzzle of the loss of public memory which was expressed in the malleability of the masses. He had in mind not only the behaviour of Fascist and Communist governments and their respective populations but, equally, the flexibility of Communist intellectuals in Britain in following shifts in the Party line. The problem such an account presents is, how can an individual escape the imposed arbitrary conventions and come to be guilty of 'thought crime' (cf. Shippey 2016: 229–254)?[5] Shaver's world independently confronts the same problems: a version of Newspeak and the paradox of thought crime, made all the more complete by a belief in a one-to-one correspondence between thought and word (Mantong).[6] Orwell struggles with the problem of narratological clairvoyance throughout his text; Shaver's narrator can only gain his insights through a sequence of teachers who already possess this double perspective, who allow him to step outside the illusions produced by the hidden masters, in the process stepping outside time and presenting both the inside view and the external perspective, illusion and truth, to the reader.

5   The same problem is present in Huxley's *Brave New World*; Shippey (2016: 239) suggests Wells' 'The Country of the Blind' (1904) is the prototype of this 'enclosed world' problem.
6   This view is shared by Orwell – see the 'Appendix on Newspeak' in Orwell's novel.

The dispersion and reintegration of forces

Kripal draws attention to the disparate attitudes of Shaver and Palmer, the one focussing on the deceptions and malice of the deros and their rays, the other pursuing a series of more metaphysical concerns and hopes (Kripal 2011: 101–106). Yet within Shaver's text the multiplication of threats and apparent lack of any central authority is countered by the role of a single system of surveillance and control, gathering and communicating information. The whole story articulates around a metaphysical dualism, the question of who in reality controls the system of information and government. Just as the Nortan civilization and space fleet is embodied in the intelligence and goodness of its leaders so, it emerges, the deleterious forces and spread of evil practices have their focus in 'ex-elder Zeit, of Atlan'. The Nortan forces win the final battle because their technicians take over Zeit's command and communication system.

Zeit is finally run to ground, a 'three-hundred footer', a 'vast mountain of flesh … not only big, but amazingly fat from his soft life in his hideout'. He is a parodic version of the Titans we have met previously, repulsive rather than attractive. We learn something of his previous history; he was exiled for trading slaves, and in his exile has sought to exact revenge on the ruling Council which dealt with him perhaps too leniently. Once captured, however, he is not destroyed, for 'that huge and evil head might contain technical secrets of value'; Mutan suggests that he is destined for torture, to repay that inflicted on the Atlan elders and the citizens.

Although Mutan has come to realize the weakness of the existing system of government, he has no alternative to propose to technologically organized centralized power. The key term in this dualist account is the virtue or evil of the rulers. In the rapidly told ending to the story, the Nortan troops first frustrate the abandondero attempts to kill the population and then clear up resistance, while the enemy are allowed to escape into space in the migration ships. The Nortans set up a temporary government composed of surviving Atlan elders, to oversee migration to a 'cold planet, far away from any sun's evil influence'. There is no suggestion of radical social reform, of a more dispersed form of government for the citizens by the citizens. Such a utopia would only distract from the purpose of the narrative which is, I believe, to offer a quite detailed analysis of the contemporary society experienced by the readers, and to reintegrate its contingencies into some version of normality. Shaver's account is a conservative version to challenge Suvin's and Jameson's socialist utopias. This feature explains the immense popularity of Shaver's story.

A society governed through information

In 'I remember Lemuria', we are offered an analysis that resonates with American society at the end of the Second War. The description integrates such elements as the place of advanced technical knowledge and a ubiquitous media in the business of government, the formation of citizens in such a society and the importance of consumerism in their lives, and the largely unremarked roles played by human sexuality, policing, drugs, the arts and preparedness for war in the background of this social order. The account takes a characteristic prophetic form (if we follow Brueggemann 1987), speaking of the reality behind appearances, expressing grief at that reality and, nevertheless, offering hope of redemption.

The key to this account is the notion of a society organized through modern information technologies. Although Shaver appears preoccupied with rays of many kinds, he is in practice talking about the communication of information and drawing attention to the political forms that accompany a society structured by information rather than by language.

Shaver assimilates radiation to this picture as the original source of information in the story, randomly dispersing both good effects – the vitality associated with exd – and bad – illness, degeneration and death linked to detrimental energy – to the individual and collective society alike. Society's task is the technical control of these effects for good or for evil ends, shaping culture man in the laboratory or deros by the abuse of stim rays in the tunnels, monitoring and informing citizens or spying on and tormenting them, put to the purposes of a quasi-omnipotent beneficent government or to those of a hidden conspiracy.

In short, in a world in large part constructed through flows of information and controlled by technicians, the motivation behind the organization of society is taken to be either compassion or malice; this is a thoroughly social view, for the condition of the other (their well or ill-being) is taken to be the overriding concern of the rulers and, presumably, of their operatives; functionally, we might note then, deros are the equivalent of Titans, not of humans. Egoism – the first of Schopenhauer's motives – appears almost forgotten as a social force, appearing only in the pleasures of the citizens or the orgies of the abandonderos, permitted by their respective chiefs.

The organizing theme of Shaver's story is then the social possibilities contained in new forms of media, notably of radio and of film and television, through which a seemingly complete record of the sounds and sights of life can be made and stored, transmitted and subsequently recovered. These possibilities are quite distinct from those available to an earlier generation who had only the written word. There is then a certain irony in Mutan's task of producing inscribed 'telonium message plates' for future generations to read, for his narrative describes both the positive consequences of such shifts in the means of recording and transmission and their potential for serving the ends of deception and manipulation. The remainder of the section is given over to exploring these implications.

First among these consequences, there is the crucial role of technicians who manufacture and control the rays that mediate information, protecting, stimulating, teaching, forming and monitoring every aspect of individual and collective life. Industry and government in effect become united in the class of technicians, forming a meritocracy.[7]

Second, with technical control there comes a need for centralized government, as much to construct the necessary infrastructure as to determine the direction of progress. Mutan is most articulate on this topic: during the capture of the 'telemechro center', which coordinates monitoring citizens, communication between technicians, and active intervention both in telecasts and in more direct form ('the police corrective ray'), he reflects on the 'centralizing of all power by the rodite [technical] method of government' and the vulnerability to takeover this centralization has created.

A third consequence is the complete separation between the technical and ruling class on the one hand and the citizens on the other. This

---

7   cf. Michael Young's almost contemporary satire, *The Rise of the Meritocracy* (1958).

separation is embodied on Mu by a distinction in kind between Titans and their creatures, which serves to naturalize the power relations. As Roth points out, late nineteenth-century racial theory forms the background to this aspect of the story and, although Mutan portrays an easy fellowship among the students of various origins, the destinies of a Titan and of a culture man are quite different in terms of the powers and responsibilities they may expect. Mutan is quite content to settle for a common life with another 'hybrid', created like him by technicians, and proud of the recognition of the contribution he has made given by his superiors. Race is destiny.

The life open to ordinary citizens is one of consumerism, of pleasure and drugs with, at the highest, the possibility of self-improvement. Participation in political life is limited to taking in the productions of the new forms of the media; they cannot join the ruling classes, and Mutan's exceptional foray into political life leads only to the restoration of a version of the existing order.

Despite this conservatism, a fourth consequence is an awakened mistrust, when evidence appears indicating this benign relationship between rulers and ruled has broken down, and paranoia becomes a substitute for political participation. If the theme organizing the story is a commentary on the potential for secrecy of a society organized around communication, it is wrong to reduce this mistrust to an expression of mental illness; rather, as suggested above, paranoia is a social response to this kind of modern society based on information.

The paranoid style

Richard Hofstadter, who coined the term 'the paranoid style in American politics' in an essay in 1963, supports this contention, identifying a 'style of mind', somewhat to one side of a politics of class conflict, which he defines as 'the use of paranoid modes of expression by more or less normal people' (Hofstadter 2008: 4). He places it in a longer-term perspective, citing examples from the late eighteenth century on, concerning fears of essentially foreign (European) conspiracies – Illuminati, Masons, Catholics – but refocussing in the 1940s on internal threats, complaining of dispossession of the citizens by elites, of internal corruption, and of the need to repossess the nation and prevent its final subversion. He elaborates its themes: 'The old American virtues have already been eaten away by cosmopolitans and intellectuals; the old competitive capitalism has been gradually undermined by socialist and communist schemers; the old national security and independence have been destroyed by treasonous plots … [by] not merely outsiders and foreigners but major statesmen seated at the very centers of American power' (Hofstadter 2008: 23–24).

Shaver's story is then a distillation of a recognizable contemporary complex, the identification of internal enemies against a global backdrop, first warfare against the Axis powers and then anticipation of the coming Cold War against Communism. Hofstadter identifies three elements in this complex: first, the notion of a conspiracy to undermine free capitalism, bringing the economy under the direction of the federal government, paving the way for socialism or communism; second, the contention that the top level of government has become infiltrated by communists, so that national policy is dominated by men selling out national interests; and third, the idea that the whole country has become infused with a network of enemy agents, active in such areas as education, religion, the press and the mass media, whose aim is to paralyse the resistance of loyal citizens (see Hofstadter 2008: 25–26). Shaver does not focus on the economy (barring mention of 'the total wealth of the planet' being stolen), but he describes the central control of society by government, the latter being taken over by alien interests, and the concealment of this displacement of power by such institutions as entertainment, education, the arts and the media.

Hofstadter dates this shift closely to the War years (1939–1945), though the paranoid mind-set can project back its account of betrayals – economic, political, cultural and military – to earlier years. He identifies its dominant characteristic as a combination of attention to detail with a crucial lack of judgement (cf. Barrow's account of appeals to immediate experience, premature generalizations and imponderable universals in the plebeian moral imagination – Barrow 1986). And he notes the amassing of evidence, the scholarship indeed, of the paranoid style, but sees the essential as 'the curious leap in imagination that is always made at some critical point in the recital of events' (Hofstadter 2008: 37). Plausibility is gained through the accumulation of facts, which is then claimed for the most fantastic conclusions.

He therefore sees the paranoid style as a 'secular and demonic version of Adventism' (Hofstadter 2008: 30). It sees conspiracy as the motive force in historical events: 'History *is* a conspiracy, set in motion by demonic forces of almost transcendent power' (Hofstadter 2008: 29), and cannot be defeated by normal political means, but only by a crusade spoken of in apocalyptic terms. The paranoid leader is therefore a militant, unprepared to compromise, seeking to eliminate the enemy, who is a 'perfect model of malice' – a free agent apparently outside historical constraint, willing the events of history, controlling political power, structuring press representations, influencing minds through seduction and education and other (paranormal) means.

As Hofstadter points out, the paranoid style imitates the supposed enemy (just as anti-cult groups behave like cults – see Shupe and Bromley 1980), adopting scholarship (and pedantry) as a means of discovering the truth, forming secret societies, emulating the commitment, discipline and organization of their imagined opponents, eliminating dissent, engaging in sensual fantasies, and subordinating means to ends. All these features appear in Shaver's account of the Nortans' conquest of Atlan society with the aim of restoring its former values.

His conclusion is that such imaginary politics is produced in social strata that have been excluded from practical participation in politics. In such a world, we might add, competing forms of imagination are at work within quite local contexts, negotiating boundaries and deals, and we might wonder whether this form of exclusionary behaviour is typical of the Protestant mind (cf. Harding 2000). Certainly, responsibility, if exercised, is so at a local level, and the experience extrapolated or projected to national and international and even interplanetary scales.[8]

---

8   Hofstadter's themes have been developed in later analyses of 'conspiracism', the contribution of millenarian and apocalyptic visions to American politics in the twenty-first century; see Barkun (2003) and Robertson (2016).

Means of charting reality in a paranoid world

Shaver's paranoia is focussed above all on the importance of new forms of the media as the frame in which this political life is carried out and, by concentrating on such a focus, he is something of a sociological prophet. For information by its nature introduces obscurity in a variety of ways. While an immense technical apparatus is required to gather and exchange information, and further elaboration needed to put out messages in such forms as art, architecture, broadcasts and so forth, structuring the mental and physical environment, none of the outputs reflect either the nature or the interests of the apparatus engaged in their production. These outputs present a variety of narratives, of the collective aspirations of the race, for example, or of 'the way to participation in love and joy', or of benign and compassionate government, but the motives behind their production and the interests present remain invisible.

Mutan uncovers an extreme instance of deception, of unregenerate malice masked by the surface appearance of benign and disinterested government. But his apprenticeship teaches a general lesson: in a world controlled by information, the truth can only be discovered by patient acts of deciphering; it cannot be read at sight, but only by going back in time to reconstruct the conditions of the production of narratives and revising previous understandings. The agent has actively to construct his or her understanding through acts of what has come to be called 'intelligence' work: overcoming deception, researching, piecing together an alternative to either common representations or rumour. Just as contemporary cinema indicated, in a world where it appears for the first time that everything can be recorded, nothing can be taken at face value.

The further implication of this lesson is that every account is a partial account, a construction emerging from a personal apprenticeship. And if one adds in the power of the 'semiotechnical' structure (Kittler 2013) to manipulate information retrospectively and prospectively, through drugs, the altering of records, hypnosis, the revision or 'recovery' of memory, and so forth, it is possible to reach a position of extreme scepticism, from which one might escape only by returning to what experienced people hold collectively to be the case. But although Shaver mentions several of these possibilities, he does not explore any of the paths leading to relativism, scepticism, or collective representations.

We might then conclude, following Peters (1999), that communication is largely experienced through its frustration and failures, when attention is misdirected, crucial information is withheld, or private conversations are overheard. It is not surprising, then, that the imagined remedy to this situation is the aspiration to direct mental communication between minds, ideally without recourse to technology which, nevertheless, offers the models for this kind of bodiless transfer. Direct inspiration – 'religious' experience – is the typical aspiration of the age of total communication. We are offered a series of instances of telepathy.[9] It begins with Mutan's sensitivity to the hidden fear in Titans' minds (acknowledged by his teacher) and progresses to the intuitive cooperation of the companions in their escape from the thought-monitoring rays of their enemies. It only reaches full expression in the Nortan civilization, however, who exhibit telepathy in the participation of the Nortan maids in Princess Vanue's 'augmented will'. We are also offered an intriguing paragraph on the conference of the Nortan Elders when the companions bring their news of the fate of Mu. The Elders work by thought projection in the form of ideographs, made visible by 'thought augmentors': 'they used an image language instead of words, and their talk was to me but a whirlwind of changing forms, faces, geometrical figures, maps of space and figures of orbits and many other things incomprehensible to me'.

The mention of augmentation indicates the Nortans were capable of assisting their telepathic powers by technology, and we have mentioned the maids' ability to control and interrogate the subdued abandondero monitors by mental power could be supplemented by the use of a telaug. But direct communication remains a possibility and an ideal; Mutan is at times in full mental communication with Vanue during the final battle and, in the aftermath, she rewards him in person yet at a distance by teleprojection.

In a similar fashion, Palmer's idea of 'race memories' which Shaver adopted consists in full access to the past (cf. Kripal 2011: 96–97), a communication of information without distortion or reduction. We might

9   On telepathy, see Luckhurst (2002).

recall, too, the rather crude earlier idea of an original Atlantean language (Mantong) which accurately transcribes reality in a one-to-one correspondence. If paranoia is a social condition – experienced grief responding to the realistic description of the world condition – there is also hope offered, the calling to achieve transparent knowledge and full communication through telepathic powers. And although we might have supposed the need for careful deciphering of clues, rather than reading at sight, would challenge or even disqualify the desire for direct communication, in practice we find that the first serves as a pathway to the second, so that deciphering is part of an apprenticeship of new mental powers.

This notion of such a calling is then the final, fifth consequence of the description of a society organized by communication of information.

Direct communication as vocation

The aspiration to direct communication is a feature of the call to join an elite community, elite both in the sense of enlightened and in their moral status. This calling has various aspects.

In the first place, the aspiration is associated with an idea of scientific progress; as we have seen, Shaver presents a pastiche of contemporary scientific discoveries, much in the style of Blavatsky's bricolage sixty years earlier. Natural science holds the key to both intellectual and moral progress. While Shaver makes some small play with the older physics of magnetism and gravity, which had been put to work in ideas of mesmeric influence and the direct experience of spirit minds, he places his reliance in ideas of 'rays', which link together radiation and wavelengths of different frequency in the transmission of various forms of invisible energy.

Then, scientific knowledge places its possessor above the run of common humanity. The true masters of these advanced sciences, which underlie all the technologies of communication, unite in themselves moral and intellectual qualities that culminate in telepathic abilities. These are supermen, embodied in a distinct race: the Titan is described at one point as 'the super being of all Mu and of the universe'. This race of supermen represents not only the origin and highest form of human evolution, but also the culmination of the processes of evolution: they are the future form of men as well. Here we meet with the orthogenetic principle to which Blavatsky gives expression; evolution has a direction.

There is an obvious contrast between Darwin's uniformitarianism – the positivist ideal that a single set of natural laws apply across the board – and the teleological account Blavatsky and others offer. The one generates an extraordinary variety of products, without any overall direction, the other brings heterogeneous materials into a pattern because of an overall purpose detected in the sequence (implying a cosmic mind). The first distinguishes similarities in various materials through homologies (descent) and analogies (functional responses), while the other detects correspondences, where coincidences turn out to have significance; the one relies on mechanism, the second on intention. The two are contrasted as the claims of materialism compared to the priority of mind; in this regard, the agenda has not changed since the 1880s.

In this teleological mindful perspective, there is a single explanation to the variety of the world, and it is simultaneously intellectual and moral: in short, it is intentional.[10] Although Shaver does not invoke a cosmic mind at work, shaping our ends, he supposes there to be a single principle of intelligibility in the universe and a single world history (and a single original language). It is therefore appropriate to find a single original race who communicate this principle, whose task is to educate and guide humanity, and who leave us appropriate instructions.

And there is a single calling, to participate in this coming, future race, to join a secret fraternity existing across time, sharing esoteric knowledge and gaining the means to embody it, developing the appropriate moral qualities to exercise the accompanying mental powers. The coming race is a return simultaneously to ancient forms and in continuity with a hidden past, with a vocation to save humanity and embody that saved life.

While Shaver shows a certain enthusiasm for bodies, these bodies are nevertheless etherealized, enhanced by mental communication as well as stimulated by rays; one cannot help thinking that stim rays are for the

---

10   Lovecraft plays with the notion of amoral intentionality with Nietzschean overtones and introduces an original race with only mischief in mind for humanity.

culture men, while Titans enjoy enhanced communion of minds. There are clear indications that the vocation to save humanity is linked to a dualistic desire to escape from the body and its limits, to live in a world of pure information.

In short, Shaver offers a Gnostic account of the contemporary world in 1945. This account is constructed through the effects of novel technologies of communication which convey narratives that bear no trace of the underlying forces at work. It describes this world of surface effects and subterranean causalities, a description which gained recognition from a wide readership of working people, including members of the armed forces at the end of the War, and which helped shape the sensibilities of a generation growing up with radio, film and, after the War, television. Sociologists in the period coined phrases such as 'brainwashing' (Meerloo 1956) and 'the hidden persuaders' (Packard 1957) to describe the experience of this generation, and wrote books with titles such as *The Lonely Crowd* (Riesman 1950). Though perhaps eccentric in their expression, his concerns were widely shared.

I hope my appreciation for Shaver's achievement is clear. He offered a prophetic vision of the world condition he experienced, in the sense of a contemporary understanding; he created it through a realization of the theosophical account of human ills and resources for repair and flourishing, while mobilizing a good deal of contemporary scientific material, turning it into a story told with enthusiasm and panache. Shaver's story is 'metaphysical' in the sense that it believes human history and indeed biological vitality are shaped by recognizably human concerns, displaying the marks of intention. It is paranoid, for it portrays a world that has been taken over, beneath an amiable surface, by interests that consume men and share nothing of their values and hopes. And it is Gnostic (combining the other two characteristics), for it aims at a state where people with trained mental powers might escape from the conditioning and contradictions of the body and establish unambiguous, reciprocal and total communication between minds. He offered this picture based on the recovery of a pure past, open to present experience, and brought to this world by messengers, messengers whom Americans were about to meet in their new form.

This is Shaver's contribution to the world of flying saucers.

Appendix: A study of Alfred Sinnett's *Esoteric Buddhism* (1883)

With respect to the study of Theosophy, I draw attention to three kinds of innovation in my treatment. In the first place, I point to the question of scale in Blavatsky's treatment of scientific discoveries, in the second, the intermediary role played by spirits as relays between these discoveries and the reformist aims of the movement, and third, in this Appendix, the exemplary role of a text published in 1883 in the transformation of the spirits, fitting them to their new tasks. To my knowledge, these aspects have been underplayed or neglected by writings about Theosophy.

I dealt with the first two topics in the preceding essay. Together, they constitute the heart of my argument concerning Theosophy, and give us the cards we need: in short, spirits are taken to drive a modern account of the nature of matter and the cosmos and, on this basis, to construct the pathways of evolution, which centre around the descent of man. *The Secret Doctrine*, however, is so dense and – although there is an underlying narrative – so lacking in structure that it presents practical obstacles even to sketching a clear exposition of its central ideas. We are then fortunate to have an earlier, shorter and simpler text in which the transformation of the spirits of the dead into planetary spirits can be clearly traced, together with the cosmology and account of human evolution that accompanies this metamorphosis. That is the purpose of this Appendix.

This earlier text is Sinnett's *Esoteric Buddhism*, composed from letters from the Masters, which were produced by Blavatsky by various techniques of precipitation, automatic writing and so forth, although the precise conditions were disputed. In the following sections, we pass in review Sinnett's redaction of the nature of the person and what survives after death, then, the planetary chain as the theatre for this process of continuing formation and, last, the role of these ongoing forms of life in the story of the human race, both in an evolutionary perspective and with regard to history. Sinnett's book allows us to trace the genesis of the settlement which is our focus as it develops in the margins of Blavatsky's wider programme; much else of theosophical import is left unconsidered. This account follows a specific interest through the materials, one I would claim that is supported by the broader history of theosophical ideas, and while I make a by-no-means standard claim concerning the origin of an important part of the field of science fiction, it has its precedents (cited in the essay), although it has not been traced before, I believe, in such convincing detail. I include this study because, as well as providing the detail of the transformation of spirits into travellers from elsewhere in space, it allows us to sample and gain a flavour of the extraordinary synthesis achieved by Blavatsky and her co-writers.

I. Genesis of the text

What of earlier forms of the argument before *The Secret Doctrine*? The project of *Isis Unveiled* turned around the condition of the spiritualist movement in the United States in the mid-1870s. This is clear from the style of physical explanations offered as a basis for the overall narrative – with recourse to such notions as aether, the principles of attraction and repulsion, and correlation between planetary movements and the life of organic matter (including human life), expressed in cycles of influence – and from the place granted to Spiritualism as a sign and anticipation of the present revelation and key being offered. *Isis Unveiled* focuses on two topics, the rediscovery of the integrity of ancient learning, confirmed by the advances of modern science, and the exposure of the historical role of the Christian Church in occluding this learning. This concealment is the subject of the second volume, which describes the creation of a Christian hegemony, together with recording a counter-tradition of resistance, tracing the continuity of earlier sources by drawing on comparative religion and revisionist histories of pagans, heretics, magicians and secret societies. The volume ends by advocating the use of Buddhist and Hindu resources to supplement and correct the deficiencies of contemporary scientific understanding, deformed by its Christian history. In sum, while modern science is on the right lines, it needs to expand out of the reductive materialism it has adopted in reaction to the insufficiencies of the Christian tradition.

The text was created, in the theosophical account, by Blavatsky lending her 'astro-physical organism to the temporary usage of another and higher consciousness, by mutual consent' (Zirkoff 1972: 12).[1] While mediumship is performed in a trance, Zirkoff claims, there was in this instance no loss of personal consciousness; Blavatsky was not a medium but a 'mediator', transmitting not the spirits of the dead (or 'ex-human and elemental entities'), but 'living men who have learned … to withdraw temporarily from their own outer constitution and enter another' (Zirkoff 1972: 13) – although men who, by their training, had gained a form of immortality. However, in Olcott's more straightforward words, 'She had loaned her body as one might one's typewriter' (Zirkoff 1972: 28). In a later article (in *Lucifer* 1891, cited by Zirkoff), Blavatsky discussed the means of communication in terms of hypnosis and thought-transference, for 'Space and distance do not exist for thought … [and we find] two persons … in perfect mutual psycho-magnetic *rapport*' (Zirkoff 1972: 37). Blavatsky's theories are what we might call an upgrade on standard spiritualist ideas, offering a broader content and more detailed terminology rather than making any radical break, and the content of either form of communication, which includes teaching on how instruction is possible, asks that the hearer be persuaded of the truth of the system at the same time as learning about it. If you accept a message from a spirit, you must accept that there are spirits; if you acknowledge Blavatsky's teachings, you also accept their source in the Masters. Instruction and persuasion are one and the same.

This mode of composition allowed two forms of defence against criticism by spiritualists, philologists and others; she acknowledged the lack of order, inconsistent use of terms and errors, and so forth, accepting the errors as hers, but claiming the teachings, as coming from the adepts, as

---

1   These paragraphs draw on Zirkoff's Introduction to a re-edition of *Isis Unveiled* (1972). Questions of the passive receptivity of mediums or their active participation have been present from the early days of Mesmerism (see Méheust 1999).

not being subject to such charges. Concerning these teachings, she resisted charges of plagiarism, for her sources were concerned with the truths being proclaimed and not with scholarly conventions, and she explained 'the relatively incomplete and fragmentary nature of *Isis Unveiled* and its teachings' (Zirkoff 1972: 43) as being aspects of a progressive revelation. This revelation, in sum, was designed to make the case for occult learning, to defend the notion of hidden teachers possessing this learning, to affirm that ancient wisdom concerns all that the modern arts and sciences were rediscovering, and to make clear that much of this wisdom had in the meantime been lost sight of (see her article in *The Theosophist* VII, January 1886, cited Zirkoff 1972: 44–45). This progressive revelation allowed for the revision of concepts as followers accrued; their progress in understanding would allow further insight to be granted. In this fashion, the unchanging nature of the ancient wisdom (modelled on positivist claims of knowledge of natural laws) can be reconciled with the mutable nature of historical human understanding.

This trio of clarifications – living teachers (Adepts), not spirits, working through an active mediator, not a medium, to bring about a progressive revelation, not messages from the dead – allowed Blavatsky later to confront the main discrepancy between *Isis Unveiled* and *The Secret Doctrine*, the treatment of transmigration of souls (metempsychosis) and reincarnation, for transmigration is denied in one book, and reincarnation central to the other. Blavatsky, while admitting to a confusion of terms, said her purpose at the earlier time was to refute the followers of Kardec, who believed in the simple transmigration of souls between individuals (Zirkoff 1972: 46). And a Mahatma, Koot Hoomi, stated in a letter to Sinnett in 1881 that the purpose of the emphasis in 1877 was 'to divert the attention of the Spiritualists from their preconceptions to the true state of things' (Zirkoff 1972: 49).

A second focus of controversy concerned the shift in emphasis from a threefold conception of man in 1877 to a sevenfold one in 1888. Sinnett also received clarification from Koot Hoomi on the shift from the triune to the septenary model in a letter (Zirkoff 1972: 49–50). A third involves Blavatsky's early endorsement of Darwin's theories about the descent of man which, as we have seen, she later corrects.

Blavatsky's thinking – or that of her teachers – evolved quickly after the publication of *Isis Unveiled*, and the key text for studying that shift was composed by Sinnett from the teachings of the Mahatmas and published in 1883. While Zirkoff saw the 'plan' of *Isis Unveiled* as part of the progressive revelation of occult knowledge for our time (Zirkoff 1972: 60), Blavatsky, who remained unsatisfied with the book, later saw it as only a 'compendium of occult facts and doctrines', and as containing 'revelations of natural facts, and illuminating thoughts and sidelights on the mysteries of Nature never suspected before' (Zirkoff 1972: 59); it is a testimony to a stage in her development of Spiritualism into an occult cosmology, and needed supplementing and developing.

The place of Sinnet's Esoteric Buddhism regarding Blavatsky's project

The ideas that appear in *The Secret Doctrine* were first outlined in Alfred Sinnett's *Esoteric Buddhism* (1883). Their source was the letters Sinnett received from the Mahatmas, outlining a synopsis of the history of the Universe. Sinnett had quoted from the first of these letters in *The Occult World* (1881), introducing his principal correspondent, an Indian sage named Koot Hoomi. Contemporary reviewers, we might note, had focussed on Koot Hoomi's American English and limited sources – they identified Bulwer-Lytton's novels and *Isis Unveiled* – and had criticized Sinnett's credulity (Meade 1980: 233). There were in all one hundred and twenty letters written between 1880 and 1884 (see Barker 1924); *Esoteric Buddhism* is based on sixty-nine of these, received in 1882.

The 'Mahatma Letters' include an account of how the writing was 'precipitated' and how transfers of letters were made in both directions (other spirit communications in this period also contain discussion of the physics allowing contact to be established – cf. Theobald 1887). The letters are from several different correspondents (Adepts), using different styles of communication, and the calligraphy varies considerably (see Meade 1980: 464–466). Their authenticity has been much debated; Meade's conclusion is that Blavatsky wrote the letters. Whether it was her conscious self at work, or evidence of multiple personalities (an emerging trope of the period), or the sources she channelled, seems of minor importance. Sinnett's book is clearly part of a series leading from *Isis Unveiled* to *The Secret Doctrine*, an instance of inspiration or intellectual ventriloquism depending on the perspective taken. We may remark that Blavatsky devotes several pages in *The Secret Doctrine* to correcting aspects of Sinnett's theories; the process of development was on-going. Sinnett's work, then, was the product of an amanuensis, and the authorship lies either with the Adepts themselves, with Blavatsky as their conscious collaborator and scribe, or with Blavatsky herself. It is an intermediate form between *Isis Unveiled* and *The Secret Doctrine*, marking a stage in the emergence of Blavatsky's mature account. The significance of the book is that we can follow the transformation of spiritualist ideas into Blavatsky's wider cosmology in some detail, and that is the purpose of this reading.

The book has twelve chapters, which fall into three groups. The first four chapters (1–4) offer a cosmology; they introduce the Teachers – the source of the new learning – and then review in turn the constitution of the individual, the nature of the physical world – the planets – and the history of the successive races on the planets. These three topics – the constitution and history of the person, the planets and the races – proceed according to a rule of correspondences. The heart of the work comes in the central four chapters (5–8), which are concerned with the fate of the human person after death and matters of human woes and flourishing, offering, in short, a theodicy which reconciles the vagaries of an individual life with a narrative of progress. These chapters contain innovations with respect to *Isis Unveiled*, introducing the connected ideas of reincarnation and fate (Karma) at the heart of this theodicy, and at the same time offering a reinterpretation of spiritualist phenomena. These innovations then represent the transformation of spiritualist ideas into the terms of the wider cosmology sketched out in the first third of the book, tying the transformations of the person to the wider correspondences ordering the Universe and its history. The last chapters (9–12) treat topics to support the claim that this combined cosmology and theodicy is the truth of Buddhist teaching, offering accounts of the Buddha, Nirvana, and the Universe in accordance with the synthesis outlined. This synthesis, indeed, is presented as the original and universal form of all religion and wisdom, the inner or esoteric core (transmitted by the secret brotherhood of teachers), which the last chapter seeks to demonstrate by showing that recent discoveries of modern science confirm the claims of this ancient learning.

My concern is to show how the cosmology – which includes a detailed account of the workings of the planetary system – draws on the spiritualist theodicy, articulated around a notion of reincarnation and rewards and compensations over a succession of lives, and how, in doing so, it generates one of science fiction's basic narratives.

The teachers and a sociology of secrecy

We may first remark how spirit controls turn into teachers,[2] creating a source of stable knowledge located in distant places and transmitted through secret schools, in this instance, the Tibetan or Great White Brotherhood. They possess an original, single core of wisdom which lies behind both ancient and modern learning, appearing in the religions, philosophy and the sciences. This perspective allows a synthesis of all learning to be created, for each part is an expression of this original form; this synthesis echoes the ambitions of the contemporary positivist project, that all knowledge could be assembled in a single system, organized by a few universal principles, but projects it back in time.

To participate in this learning takes more than intellectual curiosity; this is where Sinnett's (and Blavatsky's) project appears to separate from the positivist ambition, for the former demands discipline and obedience to authority, with the seeker of wisdom involved in a process of individual moral formation (although one could argue that the formation of a modern scientific mind is equally a moral process: see Shapin 2008). The teachers in Sinnett's account are not only learned but have rare moral qualities and,

2 The spirit John King became the messenger of the Brotherhood of Luxor, and critics have pointed to King's transformation into one of the Mahatmas, to whom Blavatsky owed the inspiration for *Isis Unveiled*. Johnson (1994), however, argues in detail that identifiable historical figures lie behind the personalities of the various Mahatmas.

at the same time, have gained exceptional physical and mental powers, for they know 'the mysteries of the spirit … [and] the material constitution of the world as well' (Sinnett 1972: 6). They form a secret brotherhood, made up of individuals whose dedication and character allows them such powers as clairvoyance, thought reading, mental communication, the transmission of instructions and even, on occasion, the power to convey physical 'apports' such as letters, and of translocation: visits to the ordinary world, with which, despite their withdrawal, they are concerned. For they identify and draw together an elect group to train, offering teaching, moral formation, participation in the original secrets, and the gaining of extraordinary powers, the 'knowledge and practical art of manipulating certain obscure forces of nature' (Sinnett 1972: 10). The acolyte becomes involved in this secret world and, by the powers and insight gained, becomes evidence of its reality and superiority to ordinary understandings. The idea of a Brotherhood of teachers supports a notion of progressive revelation, as further insight is granted in response to the faithful application, work and moral merit of the disciples. Progressive revelation also allows the correction and development of doctrine.

The notion of a Brotherhood derives from earlier sources, not entirely distinct from the first stirrings of the modern scientific mind (cf. Yates 1972 on the Rosicrucian Enlightenment), and the idea can be construed as an expression of the sociology of secrecy, linked to the conditions of production of unorthodox or non-standard knowledge. Such knowledge focusses around the repurposing of scientific discoveries by acts of will, normally to moral ends within a reformist and egalitarian, even democratic, framework; it can usually be characterized as 'autodidact' learning because of its conscious opposition to forms of established authority (cf. Barrow 1986). Despite this democratic tendency, this learning is expressed in the hierarchical nature of secret societies, with the inward concentration of knowledge in inner circles, the associated charismatic nature of leaders and their always-fraught relationships with followers, and the problems of contagion or the leakage of secrets with the possibilities of inappropriate use, of exploitation or betrayal to outsiders (see Jenkins 2013).

Let us look first at the revisions concerning a spirit theodicy, and then turn to the cosmological elements. A certain amount of detail is unavoidable if we are to grasp the generative effect of the synthesis and its capacity to incorporate new discoveries and perspectives, in short, if we are to understand its persuasive power.

II. Elements of a theodicy

A major innovation occurs in the second chapter, on 'The Constitution of Man', where a sevenfold or septenary scheme is introduced. The novelty is acknowledged as part of the doctrine of progressive revelation, for 'the first hints about the septenary constitution of man' were given only in an article by Blavatsky in 1881 (Sinnett 1972: 22). The sevenfold scheme allows the ordering of man's nature, the planets, and the history of humankind in a series of correspondences and allows the clarification of certain spiritualist ideas. To understand the fate of the higher and lower parts of the human psyche after death, we need to begin with the underlying account of the nature of man.

In Chapter 2, we are told that 'a complete or perfect man' would be made up of seven elements or principles (Sinnett 1972: 18–19). The first three are these: physical matter, the vitality that animates it, and the astral body that gives form to the body made up of the first two elements. All these are lower principles. The astral body is however 'vitalized' by higher elements; the first of these is the still-animal principle of will or desire but termed 'higher' because capable of union with reason and memory; these represent the 'animal soul' and the 'human soul' respectively. This brings us to five elements. As Sinnett remarks, the fifth, human principle is not yet fully developed, and the sixth element is only in embryo. This is the 'spiritual soul', towards which our nature aspires, and it in turn is drawn to the seventh element, 'spirit itself' (Sinnett 1972: 23). In another perspective, 'the sixth principle may be called the vehicle of the seventh' and, indeed, each higher principle is the fashion in which 'the One Life or Spirit' occupies each lower stage. Each of the four higher principles is then dependent upon the next level above it and has no independence or individuality (see Sinnett 1972: 23–24).

What then begins as a simple enumeration of level or 'planes' of being – physical matter, force, form, desire, reason, spirit – becomes both organized by the highest level – Spirit – and a progressive pathway, both individual and collective (as we shall see), towards union with that Cosmic Mind. In a later annotation, Sinnett says this perspective allows us to understand the human passage 'through the long series of incarnations of the human plane', with its increasing predominance of reason and consciousness's ascent to higher principles, overshadowed by the 'seventh principle of the cosmos' (Sinnett 1972: 26). Human progress is a transition through a series of forms, a series organized by its end point, the end point allowing the transition of one kind into the next and providing both direction (telos) and constraint (eliminating contingency and giving form) at every stage.

This approach can be claimed as materialist, for each of the higher four principles is material and molecular in constitution, 'though composed of a higher order of matter than the physical senses can take note of' (Sinnett 1972: 24). At the same time, this materialism is shaped at every stage by mind and, in the end, by the Cosmic Mind, so there is no contingency nor disorder: everything finds its place within a single scheme.

This scheme is, in short, a theodicy, as appears clearly in chapters five and six, where the fate of the soul after death is discussed. This is classic Spiritualist country, where what is at stake is revision of Christian ideas about human survival after death in the light of new ideas about the nature of matter. For the focus of Sinnett's fifth chapter is the fate of the 'higher human principles … at death … the natural destinies of each human Ego in the interval' between objective lives (Sinnett 1972: 58). And although the question of the destiny of the soul needs 'the general framework of the whole design worked out in the course of the evolution of man' to be grasped fully, we can sketch these elements in afterwards, when considering the cosmological aspects of the picture presented.

Sinnett's present concern is the fate of the higher principles, leaving the consequences for the lower to the next chapter, where he presents a new understanding of spiritualist phenomena. In the fifth chapter, the explanatory work is carried by two notions, Karma and a cycle of reincarnations, with an interval between each return. It is worth bearing in mind, however, Hanegraaff's interpretation: 'Progressive spiritual evolutionism was far more central than the belief in reincarnation *per se*. [Blavatsky] certainly did not adopt evolutionism in order to explain the reincarnation process to a modern Western audience; what she did was assimilate the theory of karma within an already-existing Western framework of spiritual progress' (Hanegraaff 1996: 471–472, cited in Hammer and Rothstein 2013: 331).

The doctrine of Karma (in this theosophical version) assumes some objective account of the 'affinities for good and evil generated by a human being during life' (Sinnett 1972: 58): it takes for granted both an objective scale of good and evil and mechanisms capable of remembering and judging, of recording and summarizing the moral effects of human actions (presumably employing a Utilitarian calculus). We are told that Karma operates through the division of the human principles at death: 'At death, the three lower principles – the body, its ... physical vitality and its astral counterpart – are finally abandoned by that which really is the Man himself, and the four higher principles escape into that world immediately above our own ... the astral plane or *kama loca* ' (Sinnett 1972: 59).

We may remark, in anticipation of the cosmological description, that just as there is a hierarchical series of seven principles comprising the human psyche, so there is a series of seven worlds organized in a corresponding fashion. What happens on this plane 'immediately above our own' might be regarded as a test or 'trial of the extent to which the fifth principle has been developed'. In other words, the human character achieved in the life just passed is subjected to judgement in the next. But, Sinnett writes, this account is insufficient as a way of speaking, in part, I imagine, because such a view suggests an external, personal judge. Instead, he suggests, the soul is subjected to an impersonal process: the sixth and seventh principles (the vehicle of Spirit and Spirit) draw the fifth (the human soul) in one direction, while the fourth (the animal soul) draws it earthwards. The fifth principle therefore contains 'superior and inferior elements', some clinging to the spiritual portions while 'its lower instincts, impulses and recollections' cling to the earthly. In short, 'the lower remnant ... floats off in the earth's atmosphere, while the best elements ... which ... constitute the Ego of the late earthly personality, the individuality, the consciousness thereof, follow the sixth and seventh into a spiritual condition …' (Sinnett 1972: 59). The human soul is sifted, and its elements parted according to their spiritual and earthly affinities, not by the act of a judge, but according to an impersonal yet moral physical chemistry. This materialist moral chemistry is significant because it allows the various ways of thinking about the person – as material, as energy, as form, as desire and so forth – to be operationalized as distinct components of the human being, which can then be treated as if they had distinct properties and an independent, objective existence, rather than simply being a way of speaking about different aspects of a single phenomenon or lifeworld.

At death, the higher human principles pass into a spiritual condition which Sinnett terms 'Devachan', drawing on a Buddhist term to distinguish the condition from Christian ideas of heaven. The discussion turns around two topics: first, what precisely of the human personality survives death? And second, what do we know about this spiritual condition in which the surviving personality persists?

Taking the first question, it turns out that what survives is twofold in nature. On the one hand, there is 'the individual monad, which survives through all the changes of the whole evolutionary scheme, and flits from body to body, planet to planet, and so forth' (Sinnett 1972: 60). We shall learn more of the monad when considering the cosmological scheme. On the other hand, there is 'man's own self-conscious personality', with regard to the same 'higher feelings, aspirations, affections, and even tastes, as it … [had] on earth'. Sinnett cites Olcott's distinction between 'individuality' and 'personality' to mark this dual nature: there is a succession of persons forming an individual chain, the chain corresponding to the monad, a line passing through 'many cyclic changes back to Nirvana' (Sinnett 1972: 61). Olcott, we learn, claims this individuality retains the memory of these previous personalities, so that an enlightened person has access to 'a permanency of records in the *Akasa*'. A person who has learned to focus on the higher principles of the psyche may in this fashion have access to past lives.

The 'Akashic record' stands for a principle of total registration and is a fitting concept for a period that saw the invention of the gramophone, film and the typewriter (to echo Kittler 1999). Techniques of total recording permit the belief that access to truth is a function of detailed, accurate recollection rather than of attention to a changing world; at the same time, they offer a guarantee of a permanent repository of learning, a kind of encyclopaedia; and they suggest that no aspect of the human personality need be lost. It may be that transhumanist claims of the possibility of downloading minds into machines, and thence into new bodies, repeats this theosophical trope from the 1880s.

Turning to the second question, we may ask what remains in this state between one life and the next? There is a clear preference for the intellect rather than the appetites: sensual feelings and tastes will drop away, but all the 'superior phases [of feelings and thoughts], even of sensuous emotions, find their appropriate sphere of development in Devachan' (Sinnett 1972: 62). Sinnett elaborates this 'subjective state' of isolation which is at the same time 'companionship with all that the true soul craves for, whether persons, things or knowledge'. Other people will exist only in the idea of them; this is an utterly individualistic heaven, and there is no notion corresponding to the communion of saints. He claims this subjective state is 'the only condition which renders possible anything which can be described as a felicitous spiritual existence after death for mankind '.

We might think such a state a bit thin, without the opportunities and constraints of relationships but only the memories or images of such.[3] But Sinnett is concerned to emphasize that this state 'is a life of *effects*, not of *causes*' (Sinnett 1972: 62–63). It is then 'not a life of responsibility, and therefore there is no logical place in it for suffering' (Sinnett 1972: 62). This allows him to separate the theosophical position from spiritualist and liberal Christian notions of the dead sharing in the suffering of those on earth, for there is no cognizance of life on earth in this state. At the same time, the idea avoids the conservative Christian supposition that all the dead wait in a trance for the resurrection at the end of the world (Sinnett 1972: 63).

We might suppose that this 'dream-life of Devachan' (Sinnett 1972: 66) persisted for ever, but, corresponding to the pattern of physical existence,

---

3 Compare the account of living with images in Bioy Casares (2003). This resemblance touches on the question of the extent to which spiritualist narratives appear to anticipate modernist literary forms. Both can be understood as meditations on the moral implications of contemporary developments in scientific understanding.

it has its own dynamic and profile over time: an accumulation of energy followed by gradual exhaustion, leading to oblivion and, not death, but birth into a new personality in objective life (see Sinnett 1972: 66–67).

Here we touch on a crux for the theory of successive incarnations. The soul in the Devachan state is isolated; though it may dream of doing good to another and of communicating with him or her, the companionship is imaginary. Communication, compassion and responsibility can exist only in the mixed state of the embodied mind; they cannot be realized or experienced in the purely spiritual state. Two observations follow from this limitation. In the first place, the material state remains crucial to the system; without it, there is no moral action, hence a theodicy is not possible, and the motive force is absent from the entire apparatus. Nirvana – escape from the material state – needs not-Nirvana to have any sense. The embodied state, which is the condition of our present (fourth) Earth life and in some sense, because material, the low point in the cycle, is nevertheless the engine driving the machine.

In the second place, because the material element is needed to allow the repeated separation of principles, the struggle epitomized in the human soul between higher and lower tendencies recurs in repeated purifications. At death, we are told, there is a period of sorting and division of the fifth principle (the human soul), before the state of Devachanic life is entered (Sinnett 1972: 73). Just as the higher principles find a subjective felicitous state in Devachan, there is a corresponding infelicitous state of Avitchi (a state of '*ideal spiritual* wickedness' – Sinnett 1972: 70), though whether this pertains to correction of a poor character or purification of elements before they are reincarnated in another earthly life is not clear to me. There is discussion of whether the personality becomes split, the vices finding one form in another human life, the virtues developing on a higher plane (see Sinnett 1972: 64–65). But in this case, it is not obvious whether there can be any continuity, nor in what the monad or individuality consists.

Sinnett's Teacher suggests that problems of this kind represent a wrong perspective: looking at matters from below rather than from the higher levels. By taking the lower approach, one misses the superiority of this understanding, which lies in its capacity to do justice to every person individually. In contrast to the Christian heaven, with its binary possibility of either admission or exclusion, and a graded series of a few options for those admitted, which are ill-adapted to the individual case, the individual finds a heaven tailored to him or herself, because 'the real heaven of our earth adjusts itself to the needs and merits of each new arrival with unfailing certainty' (Sinnett 1972: 69).

And how are evils set right? Commonplace sins reap their fruits in a following incarnation – so they are not wiped out – but serious sin is met with the 'condition of subjective spiritual misery' termed Avitchi – not eternal condemnation. Most sin, however, is punished on earth, 'its birthplace and playground' (Sinnett 1972: 71). This account of Karma also explains the 'inequalities of life' (Sinnett 1972: 73) into which we are born. There is therefore a Karma of good and a Karma of evil, centring around the event of rebirth into objective existence, and punctuated by quite lengthy periods of Devachanic existence – 'a peaceful night, with dreams more vivid than the day' (Sinnett 1972: 71).

Although Sinnett distinguishes the position he outlines from Christian ideas, it is worth remarking he has much in common with contemporary Church thinking. This is the final paragraph from Geoffrey Rowell's *Hell and the Victorians* (1974):

> Although no common, 'revised version' of Christian eschatology emerged during the nineteenth century, but rather a number of different versions, each stressing different elements in the biblical tradition in an endeavour to meet popular criticisms of the doctrine of eternal punishment in particular, there was one notable, common feature, in contrast to the eschatology of previous generations. That was the growing importance of the doctrine of the 'intermediate state'. The term itself was characteristic of the nineteenth century, and, whether it took the form of a tentative reappraisal of purgatory, or of a fore-shortened hell, or as a place of moral progress and expansion of the mind, it represented a move away from a predominantly Calvinist eschatology ... An intermediate state became important to those who wished to emphasize the necessity of sanctification before a man could attain to full communion with God. It relieved ... the problems of the destiny of the heathen and of those who had ... been deprived by their circumstances, capabilities, and environment of all reasonable chance of appreciating ... the Christian gospel. It fitted better with a dynamic, evolutionary picture of the universe, than the conception of fixed and unalterable states into which men entered at death. To some extent it relieved the tension between the judgement of the individual and the general judgement at the Last Day,

in that it could be represented as a state of preparation for the new order which was to be ushered in at the End of the World. For those who wished to recover the full faith of the age of the Fathers, it was the logical counterpart of prayers for the dead. (Rowell 1974: 215–216)

In short, Theosophy is congruent with broader contemporary Christian positions in its encounter with Buddhism.

Reimagining Spiritualism

Sinnett offers a brief classification of the possible forms of the afterlife based on this discussion. There are three options: there are souls that are going to pass on to higher levels and are formless and incorporeal; there are the spiritual shadows awaiting reincarnation on earth, which have form and objectivity but no substance; and there are the lower principles of life left as remnants, either in the form of what he calls 'Elementaries' or the results of crimes or suicides (see Sinnett 1972: 69).

Mediums may have dealings with each form. Spiritualist communications are real, but the framing of their interpretation is awry. To take the first condition, spiritualists have been puzzled by the state of Devachan, for mediums can gain visions of Devachan, although the spirits are 'unconscious themselves of undergoing such observation' (Sinnett 1972: 72). The medium's spirit enters rapport with the spirit, a blending explained as 'an identity of molecular vibration between the astral part of the incarnate medium and the astral part of the disincarnate personality'.

Sinnett turns to more detailed consideration of the other two options in the next chapter (six), offering further revision of spiritualist ideas. He first takes the fate of the inferior principles at death, where the sensation of desire as it attaches to earthly life may persist, taking the form of an astral shell, linked to the places to which its desires pertained, existing in a zone for which he borrows the term 'Kama loca' (Sinnett 1972: 73–77), a place from which some spiritual elements can in due course emerge to Devachan (Sinnett 1972: 93–94), fulfilling then some of the functions of Purgatory.

Many spiritualist phenomena relate to this 'astral shell or remnant ... [which is] a survival of volitional impulses imparted to it during life' (Sinnett 1972: 77), a remnant separated from the mediating forms relating to the 'over-shadowing spirit'. These traces of the animal soul may become 'galvanized' in a séance, gaining the ability to express its temporary consciousness in a fragmentary form through a medium, borrowing the medium's physical powers to communicate by writing or tapping (Sinnett 1972: 77–79). This so-called spirit, however, will have no consciousness in the present, Sinnett says, but is simply an echo of previous desires.

Sinnett also discusses how the limits of the medium will restrict the capacities of the astral spirit, how the spirit may borrow intelligence in answering questions not simply from the medium but from others in the circle, and how too there may be lacunae in the spirit's recollections because of these borrowings. He also notes that, for these reasons, the 'personality' produced by the medium will not be identical to that of the dead person from whom the shell has come. Further, the astral remains of those who have died prematurely and unprepared – by violence, or suicide, for instance – will remain more closely knit together and may have a stronger earthly presence, for good or evil, than the spirits discussed so far (Sinnett 1972: 83–85). These last represent the third option introduced above.

In all these instances, the spirit phenomena being explained exhibit limited coherence and can only be disappointing in the longer term to those seeking contact with the dead. However, spirits in séance are on occasion capable of showing far more coherent behaviour and of communicating in a seemingly intelligent fashion with the living. This kind of behaviour, Sinnett suggests, should be attributed to another class of agents, the so-called ' "elementals", those semi-intelligent creatures of the astral light, who belong to a wholly different kingdom of Nature from ourselves ... It is by the spontaneous playful acts of the elementals that the greatest physical phenomena of the *séance* room are brought about' (Sinnett 1972: 79–80).

Knowledge of these beings is withheld from disciples because with such knowledge comes great power. These exceptional powers begin to explain the abilities of the Mahatmas, together with the promise of occult knowledge to those they train. In the annotations at the end of the chapter, Sinnett emphasizes the importance of the apprenticeship the Masters offer, and for this reason seeks to distance his account from the spiritualist concerns or 'speculations' (Sinnett 1972: 84) of the chapter. Theosophists should move their focus from study of 'the state of existence next following our own ... [to] the broad design of Nature throughout those vast realms of the future' (Sinnett 1972: 88). In short, a focus on personal survival becomes integrated into a theodicy based on the orderings and correspondences of a cosmological system.

In this perspective, the dissociation of the elements of the human soul – known as the 'second death' (Sinnett 1972: 89) – should be understood as part of the progress of the Ego towards higher levels, and that progress may indeed be hindered by any preoccupation of a spiritualist kind, which is concerned only with the processes of recycling the lower elements to the 'general reservoirs of matter of the order to which they belong' (Sinnett 1972: 94–95). We might notice, however, that a theodicy must remain personal to a degree to succeed; there is little comfort or intellectual satisfaction in one's personal state becoming dissolved into an account of cosmic succession; spiritualist concerns remain active within the wider synthesis and at its heart, although to a degree disguised, in the notion of progression.

We now turn to consider the larger planes of existence and cycles to which Theosophy calls attention.

III. Planetary systems and planetary chains

Questions of beings on other planets and interplanetary communication appear, unsurprisingly, once attention is turned to planetary systems and planetary chains. When Sinnett outlines his planetary cosmology, the fulcrum remains the theodicy already sketched, ordered around the seven parts (and ages) of man. The cosmology provides the backdrop against which the appearance of man can be presented, and Sinnett is concerned to offer an accommodation with Darwin's contemporary narrative. Chapter three ('The Planetary Chain') indeed is presented in relation to Darwin's theory; *The Descent of Man and Selection in Relation to Sex* was published in 1871 and Sinnett's chapter supplements and adjusts the first part, concerning the evolution of man and the question of the races.[4] Sinnett begins, then, by stating that the Darwinian theory is only a small portion of the esoteric system of evolution, for 'occultists know how to explain evolution without degrading the highest principles of man' (Sinnett 1972: 28).

The first 'fact' to which this occultist theory calls attention is that 'The evolution of man is not a process carried out on this planet alone. It is a result to which many worlds in different conditions of material and spiritual development have contributed'. Many worlds are implicated in the process because human development is not simply a natural (material) process, but also has moral (spiritual) dimensions. Sinnett's starting point is a common liberal theological argument of the period: on the one hand, there are questions of justice to be answered, for it is unreasonable to suppose that man's eternal destiny can be determined by sixty or seventy years of material existence, followed by an infinite spiritual fate. On the other hand, we find that 'change, progress and improvement' is a law running through Nature, so it is probable by analogy that these principles will continue to work through future existences (cf. the remarks from Rowell in the previous section). So, we are brought to the hypothesis of 'progress through successive worlds' (Sinnett 1972: 29).

Sinnett develops the argument in terms of a planetary series, blending physical and spiritual qualities. If it is the case that 'the life and evolutionary processes of this planet are linked with the life and evolutionary processes of several other planets', then a limited and definite number of planets are necessary to 'afford Nature scope for the processes by which mankind has been evolved from chaos'. The planets 'are closely and intimately bound together by subtle currents and forces ... along [which] ... the life elements pass from world to world'. This system of worlds – which will become identified with the solar system – 'is a circuit round which *all* individual

---

4   Sinnett leaves out any discussion of parts two and three of Darwin's *Descent*, which introduce the theory of sexual selection in the animal kingdom.

entities have alike to pass, and that passage constitutes the Evolution of Man' (Sinnett 1972: 29–30).

Here we glimpse a system of planets, populated by spirits or spiritual monads, which plays a part both in the development of life on Earth and in human progress. The system of planets becomes intelligible as a place for the development of human individuality and growth: 'The higher evolution will be accomplished by our progress through the successive worlds of the system; and in higher forms we shall return to this earth again and again' (Sinnett 1972: 30).

So far, so good; we have a system of planets around which spirit monads circulate, focussed on the production and improvement of the human race. But matters do not stop there. For, just as we know that humans progress, through material forms to matters of mind, then to spiritual concerns and, finally, to participate in the Cosmic Mind so, as evolutionary progression is of a piece, future worlds will not be 'prepared for a material existence exactly or even approximately resembling our own'. Instead, there is a chain of worlds which are 'very unlike each other, not merely in outward conditions, but in … the proportions in which spirit and matter are unified in their constitution'. Each visible planet is only one of a chain; in our present world, spirit and matter are on the whole balanced (proportioned to our present human constitution), but this mix places it low on the scale of perfection. There are worlds higher along the scale in which spirit largely predominates, fit, we might guess, for these higher human-like forms, and invisible to our material sight.

As well as there being a system of planets, then, each planet also undergoes a cycle of forms. And here we meet a further refinement: the world forms preceding our own are not more material than the present earth but – because we are dealing in a cycle – more ethereal; the planetary cycle takes the form of a descent through a series of increasingly material realizations, reaching our earth as a turning point, and then ascending through an equivalent series of spiritual realizations, returning to its zero or rest point. In this fashion, the teleological shaping introduced by the addition of a final stage to the list of the elements of the human person, in the form of the Cosmic Mind, also determines the life of the planetary chain, which (we will find) comes from the Cosmic Mind, descends to the material world – our world – and will ascend again to join its source and origin. The present world with its moral dilemmas is then (as we have noted) the pivot around which the cycle of planetary forms moves, and this cycle, together with its situation within a planetary system, is the setting for the progressive evolution of each human individuality. The cosmic scheme is the vast and mobile stage for the drama of human formation and fulfilment; it is a human-centred universe.

From the perspective of the proto-human element, we are dealing, indeed, in a series of cycles, with the 'spiritual monad or entity' working its way through the cycle of a particular stage of planetary life in an order of progress, first descending from ethereal to material form and then ascending to a higher spiritual form, and then beginning 'its next cycle at the next higher stage' (Sinnett 1972: 31), making progress even as it returns to the first form of the next level. In this fashion, 'the spiritual monad performs a spiral progress round and round the series, passing ... [each time] to a higher level than before' (Sinnett 1972: 32).

It is only after many incarnations at a single level of a planet's existence that a monad passes to a higher level, and only after completing a planet's cycle through all its levels that it may pass to another planet to repeat the same formal, lengthy procedure. This simple formulation will need to recognize exceptions, as we shall see.

If this description seems unclear in parts, Sinnett remains a classic reference point for theosophists because of the simplicity and brevity of his presentation, though he has not developed a consistent terminology and several unresolved problems remain. The system was elaborated in Blavatsky's *The Secret Doctrine* (1888) and elsewhere, for example, in Besant and Leadbeater's *Man: Whence, How and Whither* (1913). Blavatsky had introduced the number seven as a constant: seven planets, each passing through seven rounds, with seven ages organizing the successive cycles of rounds, and similarly the narrative of the monads as they progress through this sequence, cycling at every stage of the planetary progression through the sequence of seven forms, from material to Universal Mind. There are other sevenfold organizations as well, notably a progression of seven races, as we shall see. It is important to realize, however, that a clear and exact system never emerges, although Blavatsky offers many instructive local clarifications. Moreover, confusing factors also emerge, for example, allowing the separation of elements from one individual and their reassembling (with foreign elements) in another unity (see the previous section). The significance of the project of systematization lies elsewhere, in such broad notions as a record or memory, which allows the transmission of gains made in one life to the successor form, and correspondences at every level between planetary and life forms, which allow programmatic claims of order and purpose and a corresponding rejection of chance. In short, despite both the details of the system and its frequent lack of clarity, the guiding thread is the overall account offered of human purposes and ends, together with an explanation of human suffering and the prospect of immortality. Let us pursue Sinnett's account.

Clarifications

Sinnett, during his early sketch of this synthesis, can also offer a series of clarifications based on this notion of a spiral of repeated progressions. In the first place, it allows him to explain certain omissions and errors in the Darwinian theory, which looks for missing links, postulates mass extinctions, and has to infer a leap from species to species. It neglects the spiral progressive character of the 'life impulses that develop the various kingdoms of Nature, which accounts for the gaps now observed in the animated forms which people the earth ... The spiritual monads which are coming round the system on the animal level, pass on to other worlds when they have performed their turn of animal incarnation here. By the time they come again, they are ready for human incarnation, and there is no necessity now for the upward development of animal forms into human forms – these are already waiting for their spiritual tenants' (Sinnett 1972: 32–33). The locus of the disagreement is whether evolution is directed by purposeful spiritual monads, produced on other planets and 'coming round the cycle in a state fit for the inhabitation of new forms', or whether we rely on the purposeless production of intermediate forms (on a single earth), resulting from 'the influence of local circumstances and sexual selection', and creating missing links of all kinds, 'animal life creeping ... up to manhood, human forms mingling ... with those of animals' (Sinnett 1972: 33).

Here the parallels with Blavatsky's slightly later writings are instructive: like Blavatsky, Sinnett's argument improvises on contemporary criticism of Darwin's theory of natural selection, concerning gaps in the fossil record, problems with the evidence for selection and adaptation, and the lack of any proposed mechanism for the inheritance of selected characters. Sinnett also proposes an alternative account for human origins: it is the result of an early return from another planet of spiritual monads, seeking but not finding human form and entering animal forms, which provokes the improvement of the highest animal forms into the required human forms, creating the so-called missing link in this fashion. In sum, 'evolution [is] accomplished ... by a *spiral progress* through the world' (Sinnett 1972: 34). This account is contradicted in certain details in *The Secret Doctrine*, where (as we have seen) further 'corrections' of Darwin's theory are presented.

Sinnett also introduces a further clarification: the 'tide of life – the wave of existence, the spiritual impulse – passes on from planet to planet by rushes ... not by an even continuous flow ... The process ... is one in which the evolution of each globe is the result of previous evolutions, and the consequence of certain impulses thrown off from its predecessor in the superabundance of their development'.

In short, here in embryo is a notion of the development of life on other planets, linked in a scheme of progressive evolution, travelling between planets to provoke new life forms on the sequence; spirit forms from another planet aid and direct human development. Sinnett, however, goes in another direction, emphasizing the vast cosmic scale of the process. If we go far enough back, to the 'fiery nebulae', the story begins with 'the elemental forces that underlie the phenomena of Nature as visible now' (Sinnett 1972: 35). We take up the process from the first world of the series, when globe A 'begins as merely a congeries of mineral forms', though the minerals are of a 'very ... subtle quality of matter', for the spirit pole predominates: they are 'the ghosts of minerals' (Sinnett 1972: 36). Receiving an impulse from elsewhere, globe A develops its 'mineral epoch', preparing the way for 'the vegetable development' and, as this period begins, passes the 'mineral life impulse' (Sinnett 1972: 37) on to globe B. In a similar fashion, 'when the vegetable development on globe A is complete and the animal development begins, the vegetable impulse overflows to globe B, and the mineral impulse passes to globe C'. Finally, the human impulse begins on globe A.

In this fashion, we learn that not only is there an interconnected planetary system, but that each planet passes through a sequence of stages, descending from the ethereal to matter and rising again to ever-more spiritual forms, and that each stage moves through a succession of kingdoms, from mineral to plant, to animal, to human (and on to spirit, and union with the Cosmic Mind). The system comprises an extraordinary orrery of cycles within cycles, and the whole forms a vast stage for the progress of monads from elementary to superhuman forms; in sum, the formation and fate of souls.

Sinnett offers yet further refinements. There are cycles of development prior to the mineral (this will allow the number of Kingdoms to rise to seven), and several waves of development in each Kingdom (pre-mineral, mineral, vegetable, animal and so forth), passing from planet to planet at the appropriate stage of ethereality or materiality, so that each monad passes around the planetary system several times in completing its mineral existence, a process repeated at each stage. In this picture, there are ethereal human forms anticipating those of this material world: 'Rudimentary man begin[s] ... his existence on globe A, in that world where all things are as the ghosts of the corresponding things in this world. He is beginning his long descent into matter' (Sinnett 1972: 37–38).

The function of this loosely sketched cosmology is, to repeat, to focus on this earth and its material conditions and, under the condition of embodied spirits, to explain the possibility of progress of human souls, both individually, through personal enlightenment, and collectively, through the history of the races. The monads are transformed spirits, and the purpose of the exercise is to extend our grasp on the causes of their ills and the means of promoting their well-being.

Because of this focus, the chapter finishes with two further comments within the perspective adopted, integrating the individual and collective concerns, and preparing for the shift to the problem of races in the next chapter. Having identified the progress of man as our concern, Sinnett adds that, not only does each monad move from planet to planet but, 'within the limits of each planet, each time it arrives here, it has a complicated process of evolution to perform. It is many times incarnated in successive races of men before it passes onward, and it even has many incarnations in every great race' (Sinnett 1972: 38). And all this progress denotes an end point, he remarks, a destination which we are only half-way towards achieving. While there is the possibility of improvement on this earth, and further gains in perfection in the other worlds of the ascending series, these can only be imagined, as occult mysteries.

In the later annotations, Sinnett revises his earlier account concerning the individuality granted the monads throughout the process; he now suggests that 'a differentiation of individualities' is part of 'a much later stage' (Sinnett 1972: 39), reserving the first evidence of individuality for the higher levels of the animal kingdom. Traces of humanity are less distributed through the entire system.

The pivot around which the planetary system turns

A narrative has emerged involving the evolution of man, his spiritual progress, and the cycle of the planets. Different stages of that evolution and progress take place on a succession of planets, each in its appropriate form so that spirits (or monads) travel between planets, each environment offering a corresponding state with matter or spirit predominating. The higher forms of life have access to and an intimate knowledge of the lower forms, though the reverse is not true, and the more spiritual forms may monitor and help the more material beings in their struggles and crises. And Earth, at the half-way point of the process, is the pivot around which the entire system turns, in the sense that the fate of the whole depends on the outcome achieved here and now. The entire cosmic process without remainder comes to a focus in the fate of the present human race, and the decisions we make will decide whether the Cosmos fulfils its purpose or not. The theosophical movement, then, with its Secret Doctrine and teachers who have access to the eternal records, holds the key to this crucial moment.

The scope of human life

These broad inferences are supported by chapter seven, which focusses on 'The Human Tidal Wave' and allows a colouring-in of man's progression or descent. While we have gained a picture of how 'the great evolutionary life-wave sweeps round and round the seven worlds which compose the planetary chain of which our earth is a part' (Sinnett 1972: 99), we find the moment of human development, meaning the stage of material realization we are familiar with and of which we are a part, can take place only in one location. We humans are to be found on the fourth planet of the series, and at the turning point (and fourth state) of the process of descent into the material and ascent into the ethereal, and at the mutation of the fourth into the fifth of the 'seven great races' through which the human kingdom passes in this round, not to mention this being the fourth of seven cosmic rounds. In sum, the present human race is the focal point of the entire process: the point up to which all cycles lead and from which they progress: our state is the point around which the system turns. This pivotal role emphasizes the moral element organizing the entire structure. Just as an individual life passes through an embodied phase, the period of moral causation, and then a disincarnate phase, where the effects of moral actions are played out as effects, so the fourth race of the fourth period of the fourth planet (in the fourth round), and the challenge of its transition into the fifth race, is the moment when morally-determined choices and actions reach their moment of crisis: it is the moment prepared for by all the earlier stages, and it will determine whether the next collective stages can be successfully achieved. Everything hangs on this time, this race, this present world. We can understand why other life in the Universe, however advanced, may be concerned with life on earth and how, despite its scale, in this sense it is a human-centred Universe.[5]

Sinnett describes the crucial distinction between active and passive phases in terms of the succession as each stage passes from one planet to

---

5   This moment of self-transparency of the system in the consciousness of an elite repeats a modern motif, traces of which are to be found in German Romanticism, modernist claims, and the modern scientific worldview.

the next; as the mid-point in each series is reached, preparation begins for the next stage on the next planet in the series, while at the same time the stage on the present planet begins to pass into obscurity. The active phase anticipates the next stage, while the passive phase sees the maturation of the effects of the first, preparing some elements for advance, and others for recycling in another incarnation.

He then applies this thinking to the planets adjacent to Earth: Mars, from which the present human-wave derives, and which is now 'in a state of entire obscuration', and Mercury, which is 'just beginning to prepare for its next human period' (Sinnett 1972: 102–103).[6] Sinnett adds a note concerning the latest evidence for the habitability of Mercury and, possibly, Saturn. He also considers the earlier and later stages in the cycle, which took place on the two planets behind Mars and which will take place on the two in advance of Mercury. But the forms of these further planets in the chain are not composed of matter that can be observed through the telescope, for they are of 'an ethereal nature ... a finer state of materiality than the earth' (Sinnett 1972: 103), being part of either the descent into materiality or the ascent out of it. The other planets visible to us, we may deduce, are then at stages of development other than that supporting the human; they exhibit the forms of the mineral, vegetable and animal kingdoms, through which each cycle of life must pass, in their realized material phase.

Owing to the 'uniformity of Nature's design', it is possible to grasp the phenomena of the life of other planets from our knowledge of the life-wave on this earth, working 'by correspondential inferences'. So, Sinnett fills out the spectrum of possible life forms by considering the history of the successive rounds of mankind; his source for this account is the revelation of the Masters, supported by materials found in contemporary sources.

As we know, 'In the evolution of man ... there is a descending and an ascending arc ...' (Sinnett 1972: 104). Each round in the downward arc is more physically intelligent than its predecessor, and each in the upward

---

6   We might note in passing that Venus, whose orbit lies between that of those of the Earth and of Mercury, has been left out of this account; planetary successions are not organized according to adjacent physical orbits.

sweep 'invested with a more refined form of mentality commingled with great spiritual intuitiveness'. In the first round, man is an ethereal being, spiritual and yet without intellect. In the second, a more physical man appears, still gigantic and ethereal, but firmer and more condensed in body, still less intelligent than spiritual. In the third round, he has developed a 'perfectly concrete and compacted body', first as a giant, ape-like creature, with increasing intelligence, while, in the later stages, his stature decreases, 'his body improves in texture', and he resembles a rational man. Notice that corresponding versions may be found on other planets, in other cycles.

These improvements continue in the fourth round, and the earliest races acquire speech. 'The world teems with the results of intellectual activity and spiritual decline'. At the half-way point of this round, the half-way point of the 'whole seven-world period is passed', and 'the Spiritual Ego begins its real struggle with body and mind to manifest its transcendental powers'. This is the present world condition.

We can now turn to prediction: in the fifth round, both intellect and spirituality advance, and the transcendental faculties develop, struggling with physical intellect and propensity. This is, of course, the challenge that confronts the theosophist. In the sixth, 'humanity attains a degree of perfection both of body and soul, of intellect and spirituality' (Sinnett 1972: 105), unrecognizable to the present period: 'supreme combinations of wisdom, goodness, and transcendental enlightenment' become the normal human type, with the mysteries of Nature (at present offered in small part by Sinnett's writings) being common knowledge. And in the seventh round, mankind will be God-like, and we cannot forecast its attributes. We might notice how this schema applies not simply to the possibilities of life on other planets – creatures from the future able (through time travel) to heal our present woes because they understand our struggles – but also mimics the hopes placed in the scientific community by the positivist worldview.

Sinnett touches finally, in this chapter, on the important – and related – issue of how certain souls can be in advance of their time, monads that outstrip their companions in development, anticipating the future kind, though he states that this excursus consists in speculations of his own and has not come from the Masters. He offers two kinds of solution. This acceleration may occur either through occult training or 'by virtue of the total number of ... [the individual's] previous incarnations' (Sinnett 1972: 106). In the annotations he touches on the power of the Mahatmas to intervene directly by accomplishing 'artificial incarnations' (Sinnett 1972: 109), presumably, the direct transfer of advanced powers to chosen individuals such as Madame Blavatsky. Here we have sketched a potential mode of operation by advanced spiritual monads from other planets, selecting individuals whom they prepare for a special role and instruct by means of inspiration such as telepathy and automatic writing. He also reflects on the potential of the remnant of a population left on a planet when the cycle of life moves on: this may not be simply a period of passive reflection and sorting of elements, he suggests, for, instead, 'the monads associated with these small colonies follow ... different laws of evolution, and ... [may] pass on from world to world along what may be called the inner round of evolution, far ahead of the race at large' (Sinnett 1972: 110–111). This process may also allow for the projection of an individual soul out of the 'great human vortex ... into the attraction of the Inner Round' (Sinnett 1972: 111). Sinnett ties these speculations to the notion of an exceptional vocation regarding the salvation of humanity, for his overall concern is how to explain exceptional individuals, ahead of their time. I mention it because it provides a starting point for various science fiction improvisations around a population departing for other planets, leaving a remnant with both advanced and backward elements present and resources each party can deploy.

IV. The Root-Races

Rather than simply developing the theme of life on other planets, Sinnett elaborates the succession of races through which the spirit monad must pass in its human stage; this is in chapter four, 'The World Periods'. While the history of the races serves as the setting for the moral progress of the individual, simultaneously, that collective, racial history parallels the individual fate: the progress of races mirrors the evolution of the spiritual monad. In short, the history of the races is a function of the theodicy of the individual spirit, just as is the organization of the planets; the correspondences have the individual spirit as their focus.

He confirms both these claims. On the one hand, the cycle of the races on a single planet repeats the cycle of the planets at a smaller scale: 'The development of humanity on this earth is accomplished by means of successive waves which correspond to the successive worlds in the great planetary chain' (Sinnett 1972: 42). And on the other hand, this succession of races provides a setting for the progressive evolution of 'the individual unit [which], having arrived on any given planet ... has to live through a series of races on that planet'.

As we have seen, these correspondences between levels illustrate 'the uniformities of nature'; Sinnett touches on the sevenfold nature of many cycles – the ages of man, objective worlds, colours in the spectrum, notes in the musical scale, (to which he adds seven natural kingdoms) – as offering evidence for 'the regular operation of the septenary law in Nature' (Sinnett 1972: 44), in order to add there are also seven races. He will also introduce a further, contrasting, concept later in the chapter, that of the catastrophe, the notion of an ending to, and pause between, each successive stage in a chain of monads, planets or races.

First, however, he is concerned to give some detail to the succession of races. Man must pass through seven rounds (progressions through seven worlds) to work out his destiny. The present round is the fourth, as we know, in which the material principle predominates. And in that round, we belong to the fifth race, a race which began around a million years ago. Further, we learn that 'each race of the seven which go to make up a round ... is itself subject to sub-division' (Sinnett 1972: 45); there are seven sub-divisional races and, moreover, seven branch races within each sub-division. There is then plenty of possibility (343 units in theory) for distinguishing and classifying the races, and we learn that 'Each individual human unit must pass [through all these racial sub-divisions] during his stay on earth, each ... round'.

We are reminded that each spirit monad spends less time in physical form than in the subjective condition between successive lives, and the distinction between the physical world of moral causes and the spiritual world of their effects is repeated, though both physical and spirit existence belong to the succession of race incarnations. Although these matters are not much discussed, we get glimpses, in this parallel between individual and race lives, of, first, the possibility of progression through a series of racial forms, second, the implication of the recollection (at some future stage) of past racial lives, and third, the ghostly potential, in the material world of effects, of cast-off 'astral dross' of previous racial forms living a 'more or less independent existence' (Sinnett 1972: 47).

Although these spiritualist concerns of immortality, recollection, and ghosts remain central to Sinnett's project, he also integrates them into a broader history of the races conceived in terms of civilizations, which we have already touched on in outline. The first and the second races, so his teacher tells him, did not develop anything that could be called a civilization, and so have left few traces. The third race and earlier stages of the fourth, however, have done so, and this perspective allows the integration of various materials drawn from contemporary scholarship, something that will achieve far higher form in Blavatsky's *The Secret Doctrine*.

This is the juncture at which he introduces the notion of catastrophes, drawing on evidence from the 'regular routine of planetary life ... [of] convulsions of Nature ... [and of] great geological changes' (Sinnett 1972: 48). Picking up the idea from contemporary geological investigations, we learn that new continents come into existence, continents on which the distinct races and their civilizations develop, to be cut off from their successor forms by 'great continental cataclysms'. There are 'seven great continental cataclysms' punctuating the history of this earth, each terminating a race at its appointed time, although leaving some survivors who, after a period of flourishing, invariably collapse into barbarism. The teacher suggests that traces of earlier cataclysms may be found in lower geological strata, that the present continents may in future sink, and – potentially – the older re-emerge (see Sinnett 1972: 49–50).

This notion of repeated catastrophes was picked up later by pulp authors as various as Lovecraft and Richard Shaver and by millenarians such as Mrs Keech and other contactees. It allows Sinnett to place civilizations earlier than those we have records of, and to improvise narratives using fragments of ethnology, prehistoric archaeology and palaeontology. Thus, the name of the continent of the fourth race, preceding our own, was Atlantis, which Sinnett links both to references in classical literature and to 'the Eocene age' (Sinnett 1972: 49). The continent of the third race, Lemuria, stretched over the area of the Indian Ocean and connected with Atlantis, but flourished and drowned far earlier, 'before the early part of the Eocene'. Relics of this third race may still be found in 'the flat-headed aborigines of … Australia', although, before decline, these earlier civilizations were not backward but, on the contrary, far in advance of 'Greek, and Roman, and even Egyptian civilization' (Sinnett 1972: 50).

These sketched-in details serve as a background to a more detailed understanding of the history of our period and race. The key to the matter is that, in the present cycle, we are concerned with the decline of the fourth race and the rise of the fifth. The teacher states that 'The majority of mankind belongs to the seventh sub-race of the fourth root-race – the … Chinaman and their offshoots … (Malayans, Mongolians, Tibetans, Javanese, etc.)' (Sinnett 1972: 52). The fourth race, as we have just learned, is also 'intermixed with the remnants of the third', and these 'fallen, degraded semblances of humanity are [also] the direct descendants of [unknown] highly civilized nations'.

It is hard to discern a clear pattern. The first sub-race of the fifth root-race, the most elevated spiritually, are the Aryan Asiatics, while 'the highest race (physical intellectuality) is the last sub-race of the fifth – yourselves, the white conquerors' (Sinnett 1972: 51–52). We are presumably dealing in the Indo-European group (and there are traces of Müller's scheme of three major language groups). The Greek and Roman civilizations and, indeed, the Egyptian, is part of 'our own Caucasian stock' (Sinnett 1972: 50), and these civilizations, which rose and fell, were preceded by the Indian, 'one of the first and most powerful offshoots of the mother race, and composed of a number of sub-races, lasting to these times, and struggling to take once more her place in history'. On the Indian model, we are offered glimpses of other great civilizations – Chaldean, Assyrian, Phoenician – earlier than the Greek and Roman and, it is claimed, there will be traces discovered of 'civilizations of the ante-glacial period' (Sinnett 1972: 51). The teacher is aware of the earliest stages because the memory of man is held in 'the sacred record of once mighty nations, preserved by their heirs', and these insights are supported by fragmentary evidence of various kinds, such as the surviving Asian aboriginal peoples, and deposits of the fossil bones of extinct animals mixed with those of domestic beasts.

What is at stake in this teaching?

This elaborate improvisation on the history of civilizations draws on several contemporary disciplines – geology, archaeology, ethnology, palaeontology – and, more importantly, reflects a moment in the self-understanding of the period. On the surface, its aim is to place 'our own Caucasian stock' in wider perspective, and it achieves this end by evaluating contemporary advances in knowledge against the horizon of progressive evolution, revealed to the reader by the teacher who draws on ancient wisdom. The notion of a series of cataclysms allows the advances of the current period to be situated and evaluated. On the one hand, we multiply the histories of man: in addition to known human history and prehistory, we invoke the civilizations of Atlantis and Lemuria with their parallel or even greater achievements and note their decline. On the other hand, we can anticipate the fate of our own civilization and the transition to further world-rounds, with yet greater achievements, within the trajectory being sketched. We can also glimpse the possibility of ancient learning being recovered and longstanding promises being fulfilled.

There is a quality peculiar to this sense of being at a hinge point in history; the time when a new sense of self-awareness emerges. The 1880s saw both a celebration of materialism in the positivist project and a dawning sense of the limitations emerging in that project. This project was possible because of the claim that all conditions may be explained by a few scientific principles of universal application, on the Newtonian model. Yet, beyond a humane impatience with all that is left out by such a reductive materialism (see Turner 1974), there was also a sense that there were scientific phenomena emerging for which the positivist synthesis failed to account. One way of grasping this concern is (as we have seen) to focus on matters of scale: mechanics accounted neither for the very small scale of atomic phenomena, nor for the sense of patterns at the very large scale. The positivist moment was accompanied by signs of the collapse of the promise of any universal ordering and the emergence of new ways of making sense. We might notice how Sinnett and Blavatsky registered this contemporary moment in each aspect, at least in outline, allowing the intermediate zone of human (racial) history to be made sense of with respect to the very large-scale phenomena of cosmic patterns on the one hand and the very small-scale phenomena of the monads on the other, and placing it all within a coherent theodicy. While their assumption that positivist-style rules apply to all three levels now appears naïve (a mark of the autodidact), their observation of the issues of different scales was spot-on. This 'matching' to the intellectual *zeitgeist* explains a good deal of the enduring charm and persuasiveness of the settlement offered by Theosophy, for it offers a map of the different kinds of knowledge emerging in the period as well as plotting a route across the new terrain.

The teaching in this chapter indeed comes to a focus around the question of what lies behind the recent 'rush of human progress within the last two thousand years as compared with the relatively stagnant condition of the fourth-round people …' (Sinnett 1972: 52), for the longer perspective provides the key to understanding our own moment. The teacher considers this recent period of progress in the perspective of 'the law of development, growth, maturity, and decline' of every race and sub-race; we are dealing, rather than with stagnation, in 'transition periods' (Sinnett 1972: 53). At present, the fourth race is beginning its downward course, while the 'western sub-race', belonging to the fifth race, is 'running on to its apex' (Sinnett 1972: 52), although the present white race is ignorant of the earlier conditions of civilization.

National and racial fortunes pass through a moral and intellectual cycle, paralleling the individual cycle (Sinnett cites Draper's *History of the Intellectual Development of Europe* – Sinnett 1972: 56–57), and the teacher draws the parallel between the planetary cycle and that of civilizations (Sinnett 1972: 53). Every culture, no matter how great and successful, will know catastrophe: on the model of Atlantis, catastrophe 'comes in its appointed time and place in the evolution of rounds', and prediction is possible 'with as mathematical a certainty as eclipses and other revolutions in space'. And the parallel with Atlantis allows more detailed comparison with our contemporary condition. The Atlanteans too had 'world men of science

... [who] had learned the secrets of the disintegration and reintegration of matter ... and of control over the elementals' (Sinnett 1972: 55). But this progress was accomplished at the price of a loss of moral judgement, failing to guard against the abuse of these powers for material ends. They were cut off by a catastrophe, leaving a remnant which flourished for a while and then declined. The warning is clear to our materialist fifth race, which is advanced in 'physical intellectuality' but lacking a spiritual civilization: despite our progress based in 'intellectual research and scientific advancement ... [and] powers over Nature', we are challenged to develop a comparable 'spiritual advancement' and an 'elevated morality' to allow us to control our materialist ambitions.

In short, the racial classifications employed – though lacking much systematic focus – are much of the period (see Barzun 1937; Stocking 1987), but the improvisations to which they are put have quite another purpose, which is to reintroduce moral criteria into the discussion of scientific practices and doubt into the certainties of the contemporary positivist mindset. This is part of a claim to authority for a new revelation: a distinct synthesis of recent scientific discoveries explaining man's place in the universe and the fate of the soul both here on earth and in the cosmos. This narrative defines a major trajectory of early science fiction. It is in the end a reassuring message for, although the self is always threatened by the scale of the cosmic processes within which it forms an infinitesimal element, those processes are themselves always accommodated to and modelled by the human person, focussed around human needs and desires and shaped in the long-term by experiences in this embodied condition. To conclude this reading, we then return to the discussion of the individual's potential and possible fate in the present period, given the extended scope.

V. A re-focussing of human woe and well-being

In the last of the first eight chapters in which he outlines his scheme, Sinnett returns to his organizing theme, 'The Progress of Humanity' (the chapter title), or, in other words, an explanation of human flourishing and the purpose of human suffering. He introduces a further refinement in his moral narrative, concerning where responsibility lies: in the first part of the cycle, the Ego is not invested with spiritual responsibility, for it is under construction and under the control of other beings, while in the second part, different principles operate, for the Ego must participate actively in the 'stream of progress' (Sinnett 1972: 112) to achieve its ends. In practice, this clarification reintroduces the figure of the advanced teacher, the Masters (which is where the account began), for the first part of the process takes place under their guidance and the second part is concerned with the progress of the Egos as they join the ranks of the Masters.

The consciousness of the Masters supplies the memory of the system and constitutes its coherence, and, in this fashion, the Masters mediate the Cosmic Mind, which is expressed at every level of organization, from atoms to planetary systems and beyond. In this way, too, nothing is lost through contingency, and everything recorded; we learn for example that the advanced Egos of the sixth and seventh rounds are 'identified by an uninterrupted connection with all the personalities which have been strung along that thread of life from the beginning of the great evolutionary process' (Sinnett 1972: 113). The two organizing principles of progress and memory are reconciled in the just minds organizing the whole process in every detail.

Despite the immense scope of the whole process both in time and space, this active reconciliation of principles focusses on the present moment and this earth, for we are at the hinge between the earlier and the later rounds, between then the tutelage of the earlier races and the 'period of full growth', when a man's choices will 'enable ... the continuous Ego also to make its final selection'. Sinnett elaborates his argument: 'we are coming now into the possession of the faculties which render a man a fully responsible being, but we have yet to employ those faculties during the maturity of our Ego-hood in the manner which shall determine the vast consequences hereafter' (Sinnett 1972: 113–114).

This present moment – 'the first half of the fifth round' – is the moment of judgement, when the Masters (or the Principle they embody) begin to select out the pupils who may join their number, according to their progress. Sinnett points out, however, that this selection is not precisely on moral grounds: the struggle we are engaged in is conceived less in terms of that between good and evil and more as 'the ever-recurring... conflict between intellect and spirituality' (Sinnett 1972: 114). Theosophical teaching redefines what is at stake in the theodicy it presents, which is less a moral matter and more to do with certain mental properties and with what I shall call 'direct inspiration' and its reception.

For in this teaching spirituality is defined as to do with 'the capacity of the mind for assimilating knowledge at the fountainhead of knowledge itself – of absolute knowledge – instead of by the circuitous and laborious process of ratiocination'. The contrast is between unmediated experience or intuition, knowledge communicated directly by occult sources, and the careful construction of understanding, with all its delays and detours, by unaided human procedures. This distinction, we might notice, anticipates William James' thesis in *Varieties of Religious Experience* (1902) and, like him, draws on models of mental processes given form in Mesmerism, Transcendentalism, Spiritualism and New Thought.

Discussion

It is worth pausing for a moment to consider what Sinnett conceives to be at stake in this distinction. He suggests that intellect, in the sense of ratiocination, is a European product, and leads to the depreciation of spirituality. The powers of the intellect arise through the cultivation of the physical sciences, while the threat it offers arises through its neglect of the cultivation of spiritual existence. If, he continues, the periods between incarnations (the devanchanic periods) exceed man's periods of physical existence by a ratio of 80:1, 'intellect is in error when all its efforts are bent on the amelioration of the physical existence' (Sinnett 1972: 115). Put in more extreme terms, the choice is not one between wickedness and virtue in this physical plane, but between whether a man simply lives a physical existence and then ceases to exist, or whether he continues to exist beyond this plane. This at-first-sight curious argument places the question of the survival of death and immortality, together with the associated problem of just desserts and compensations for suffering in this life, at the centre of any scientific project, and draws attention to the limits of this project. We might briefly note the wider context of such an argument, however curiously it is phrased.

Sinnett has no interest in the intermediate scale of language, at which specific groups of humans interact to construct limited projects, moving instead to considering the two contrasting scales of the very large – the Cosmic, or 'the point of view of the Universe' (Sidgwick) – and the very small – that of personal responsibility for the cultivation of the self – and to the possibility of direct communication between the two. In making this choice, he moves from language to what we would now call 'information' as his dominant concern, and from a temporality of delay and the construction of understanding after the event to an instantaneous co-presence of knowledge between the Cosmic and the personal levels. In both respects, the occult model resembles the ideology, though not the practice, of its contemporary scientific worldview. In making this shift, Sinnett is part of his period, replicating tropes that appear both in contemporary philosophy and the natural sciences (see Peters 1999). The dream of complete communication between one moment and another – the accurate transfer of information without distortion or remainder – was supported by new technologies of the time which exploited the recording, storage and transmission of sound and light waves, by the gramophone and in film. At the same time, these new technologies depended on recent scientific discoveries that contributed in time to the collapse of any simple mechanical account of nature, undermining the positivist ambition of a total description of the universe. A range of contemporary accounts of ethical practice share affinities with these technical shifts.

Returning to Sinnett's focus on his theodicy, we may note some unusual features. Virtues and vices fall to a secondary level, determining happiness and misery, but 'not the final problem of continued existence' (Sinnett 1972: 116). Within the perspective of spiritual existence, the crucial distinction is between progress and extinction, for 'ultimate progress is determined by spirituality irrespective of its moral colouring'. This speculative passage leads to a dualistic conclusion: immortality may be one of two kinds – identification with God or with Satan. Anything in between vegetates and dies without remembrance, being (he is citing Eliphas Lévi) 'the useless portion of mankind' (see Sinnett 1972: 117). These ideas bear on 'the final sorting out of humanity at the middle of the great fifth round, the annihilation of the utterly unspiritual Egos and the passage onward of the others to be immortal in good, or immortal in evil'. The lukewarm, he states, will be spewed out (here echoing the Book of Revelation).

This passage would merit extended comment. We have, in the first place, the timely appeal of Theosophy, for we are entering the vital period, just past the turning point of the entire cycle, when a version of the final judgement is enacted, sorting those monads which are to gain immortality from those which perish. Then, there is the importance, in this process of judgement, of direct communication, experienced as intuition or inspiration, modelled on features of contemporary technologies, and implying the purging of all those who rely on mediated knowledge alone and deny the authority of the Masters. This is a version of election which nevertheless demands that the elect respond through participation and work, both anticipating and responding to the momentary gifts of insight. In short, this is a lifeworld which combines millenarianism and self-making. And last, there is the Nietzschean acknowledgement that morality is secondary to immortality, a position which allows, on the one hand, the identification of 'light' and 'dark' lords, Masters of both kinds, at work in the history of the society and of the world (a motif that is developed in the period of Leadbeater and Annie Besant, after Blavatsky's death) and, on the other hand, the exploitation of the dark path to power as well as the light path, a possibility that was explored by a range of occult experts and magicians in the twentieth century (see Owen 2004b).

Although none of these three features is original to Theosophy, in this combination we are close to the heart of Blavatsky's transformation of Spiritualism into a unique synthesis, minor in some respects but with a moral and intellectual cogency that has lent it a wide plausibility, during which spirits have become, almost by accident, interplanetary beings.

The sixth sense

Given these motifs, it is clear why Sinnett focusses on the production of the spiritual self in the present in his conclusion to the chapter, describing the exact feature defining the Magus or superman (or spaceman) who may result. It is not altogether a reassuring picture. His account is organized by an occult epistemology, for spirituality (in the occult sense) means 'tak[ing] cognizance of the workings of Nature by direct assimilation of the mind with her highest principles' (Sinnett 1972: 117). While the physical intelligence relies on the five senses as the only avenues to consciousness, there is evidence (such as clairvoyance) that man has a potential further faculty 'capable in its highest development of leading to a direct assimilation of knowledge independent of observation'. This is a potential 'sixth sense', allowing the direct apprehension of knowledge, associated with an advanced nature.

Occult training is concerned with developing this faculty, which then conveys the truths portrayed in Sinnett's book; adepts produce 'mental pictures in our dormant sixth sense' (Sinnett 1972: 118), learning (for example) about details of the complex nature of the planetary system. Again, it is worth remarking that the learnt techniques of producing mental pictures are taken over from spiritualist (and other) practices, and may include, beyond attention to mental impressions, automatic writing and spirit voices.

The sixth sense is intended for wider use in future states, for each round is devoted to the development of a specific human principle. We return to the structure of the person with which we began: first, the body is developed, then, vitality and, after that, we may presume, the astral body (though Sinnett omits mention of this stage from his list). In the fourth round, we develop will and desire and, in the fifth, reason and intelligence. As we have learned, 'in the fifth round, the completely developed reason, intellect, or soul, in which the Ego then resides, must assimilate itself to the sixth principle, spirituality, or give up the business of existence altogether'. This assimilation may be correlated with Buddhist talk of the soul's union with God, and the development of the sixth principle at this stage, as it were prematurely, allows the successful negotiation of the dangerous period of the latter part of the fifth round, when the principle of reason might predominate and terminate the process. While this faculty is exceptional at present, it will become 'the ordinary business of Nature' (Sinnett 1972: 119) in future, as the will evolves and finds union with the final purpose of Nature.

Sinnett finishes his summing up of the new theodicy offered by Theosophy, which we might construe as the integration of the point of view of the Universe into the world of personal concerns, by noting the costs of such a shift in perspective, explaining why someone might be willing to pay them and how, in practice they are mitigated. A good deal of material, he agrees, is lost at each stage: 'a great many human Egos … never pass through the trials of the fifth round' and, moreover, 'it is inevitable that a great deal of the free-will evolved should turn to evil, and … be dispersed and annihilated' (Sinnett 1972: 120). Yet, these processes need to be understood in perspective; on the one hand, we should not be so concerned with the consequences for single lives and, on the other hand, we can understand both the extraordinary advances that are possible in a single earthly life and – significantly – the lasting consequences that such advances contribute in Nature.

This overriding focus on the importance of decisions made in the present life resembles certain tensions in the older, Protestant position; the effects of this brief material existence are longstanding in the spiritual sphere. As we learnt at the outset, to endure, the present person must develop in the spiritual direction and overcome the attractions of the material. Nevertheless, despite the clear-cut alternatives offered of participation in the purposes of the Cosmos or annihilation, Nature permits many retrials and incarnations. Only if an Ego is simultaneously both attracted to matter and repelled by spirituality is it 'to die … without remembrance' (Sinnett 1972: 123), and even then (we learn from the annotations) it may be recycled in the next planetary existence; in this sense, judgement (and annihilation) is never eternal.

In sum, the scheme concerns education in terms of intellectual understanding, with moral grace notes rather than formation in terms of character. This is an elitist perspective, despite the democratic offering that anyone may participate; the process of education begins under guardianship, proceeding to responsibility for one's own education in the present period, leading to a position of being able consciously to participate in and embody the opportunities available. The alternative is to choose the material path, leading either to annihilation or being returned to the educational cycle (Sinnett 1972: 124). One becomes a 'perfected being', a god, in the next age, or else is recycled.

VI. Theosophy's relationship to Buddhism

One question remains: why is this theodicy called an 'esoteric Buddhism'? Despite the use of a range of Eastern terms, none of Sinnett's account so far depends on non-western ideas; it is, rather, a transformation of spiritualist concepts, drawing in part on the system found in Andrew Jackson Davis's reading of Swedenborgian notions (see Albanese 2007), and playing with consonant mechanistic themes which emerge from reading about contemporary scientific advances. What do the remaining chapters (9–12), on Buddha, Nirvana and the Universe, add?

We may follow Prothero, who points out in his study of Olcott's Theosophy that we are dealing with 'a Buddhist lexicon informed by a Protestant grammar' (Prothero 2011: 69; cf. 9, 101–106). In Sinnett's case too, the various Buddhist terms allow him to illustrate and clarify his theodicy. Thus, the point of the qualifier 'esoteric' Buddhism is that it allows him to correct and develop 'exoteric' Buddhist ideas, those shared by contemporary practitioners or collected by historical scholars such as Müller or Rhys David. Theosophists are not bound by Eastern thought; rather, they find in Asian religions and philosophy sources that reflect and confirm the 'original' texts and teachings to which they have privileged access. In this perspective, the Buddha represents the type of the teacher, embodying the sixth principle by which 'a man has ... the power of guiding his own Spiritual Ego ... after he has quitted the body ... it is quite within his power to select his own next incarnation ... He becomes one of the conscious directing powers of the planetary system to which he belongs ...' (Sinnett 1972: 128). The history of Buddhism is retold in this vein: the Buddha is one of a series of such incarnations, to whom a sequence of reforms may be attributed, and the history of distinct schools traced. In this fashion, the history of Buddhism is assimilated to the task of establishing the authority of the Tibetan school, which is claimed as the writer's source.

In a similar way, the doctrine of Nirvana is recast to support the state of enlightenment to which discipleship leads, allowing Sinnett to distinguish such a path from the Christian faith. 'It is by a steady pursuit of, and desire for, real spiritual truth, not by an idle, however well-meaning, acquiescence in the fashionable dogmas of the nearest church, that men launch themselves into the subjective state, prepared to imbibe real knowledge from the latent omniscience of their own sixth principles, and to reincarnate in due time with impulses in the same direction' (Sinnett 1972: 148). One doctrine is not, then, as good as another, and the western intellect must adapt itself to the pursuit of discipleship and to the development of the inner faculties, by which alone truth and knowledge may be 'cognized with certainty' (Sinnett 1972: 149). Free enquiry and empiricism will not serve.

As well as distancing himself from Christianity, Sinnett then also separates his project from the methods and mental approach of the contemporary physical sciences. This is the object of the discussion of the Universe. Because there is a balance between the progressive sequence of cycles, on the one hand, and intervals of total rest, even annihilation, on the other, everything depends on the mechanism that calls for the 'resumption of arrested activity' (Sinnett 1972: 151) and that allows for the transmission of memory across these periods of silence. The active forces calling each successive stage into being are the higher spirits, themselves expressions of a generative principle, a First Cause or Cosmic Mind. He attempts to give this principle a content: 'The one eternal, imperishable thing in the Universe … is that which may be regarded indifferently as space, duration, matter or motion' (Sinnett 1972: 153). Yet he immediately distinguishes the insights of occult science from those of the natural sciences, for the former are supplied by 'endowed representatives … commun[ing] directly with beings as much greater than ordinary mankind as man is greater than the insects of the field' (Sinnett 1972: 154). Occultists, indeed, deal in natural law '*plus* the guiding … of the highest intelligences associated with the solar system … the perfected humanity of the last preceding [aion]' (Sinnett 1972: 155). These latter figures guide planetary evolution, operating through the limits of Nature's laws and within the moral law of man's free will.

These advanced teachers, planetary spirits, allow the scientific and moral spheres to be brought together and to serve one end, that of progressive evolution. And they serve a self-revealing, self-directing Mind. The moral ends of man at the small-scale match with the laws of nature at the large scale, for both are organized – through intermediaries – by the Cosmic Mind. The claim on behalf of esoteric science is then that its representatives understand the 'enormous areas of time and space in which our solar system operates', and can explore it, because they understand that 'everything is accounted for by the constructive will of the collective host of the Planetary Spirits, operating under the law of evolution that pervades all Nature. They commune with these Planetary Spirits', learning the laws which apply to this as to other solar systems, for 'the law of alternating activity and repose is operating universally' (Sinnett 1972: 157).

The Buddhist terms have quickly given way to a series of western concerns, placing the new knowledge with regard to the Christian religion and emerging scientific discoveries, replicating the organization of *Isis Unveiled* in miniature. We are offered a materialist account, one in which Spirit is expressed through 'matter, space, motion, and duration' (Sinnett 1972: 159), which unites science and religion and brings Earth and Heaven into relation in a revision which takes account of the perspective within which human life now must be viewed. In brief, the problem confronting humanity is the vast scale of the universe that is emerging, both in space and time, and our human place within it.

This focus on temporal and spatial scale is confirmed by the final chapter, 'The Doctrine Reviewed', which falls into two parts, a review of moral questions in the light of the insignificance of the stage of life on earth in the whole scheme of things, and the confirmation of esoteric doctrine offered by the most recent scientific discoveries. Sinnett returns to questions of moral equivalence and justice, construed along consequentialist lines, reiterating the matching of processes at the different scales of the micro- and the macrocosm. He invokes correspondences with the 'observable facts of Nature' as a means of checking esoteric doctrine (Sinnett 1972: 168), mentioning geological evidence of continental upheavals and floods on the planetary side, and evidence drawn from the descent of man and embryology as supporting the cycles of ages and races (Sinnett 1972: 170f.).

In sum, 'esoteric Buddhism' combines a single principle, natural laws, and higher purposes: 'we find a sublime simplicity, like that of Nature herself – one law running into infinite ramifications – complexities of detail ... however unchangeably uniform in her purposes ... always the immutable doctrine of causes and their effects, which in turn become causes again in an endless cyclic progression' (Sinnett 1972: 181).

What have we learnt?

Four things emerge from reading Sinnett's account of the structure and history of the universe.

First, we have seen how the spirits of the dead are projected onto the interplanetary scale and how their properties are transformed in the process.

Then, it becomes clear that the figure of the individual, made up of a series of layers, remains at the heart of the description and, as a consequence, the working of the entire universe is explained by phenomena at the human scale and with the aim of fully realizing humanity's potential.

Third, following from this, the workings of the universe are coming to a crisis in the present period and in this present, earthly location, for the earth at this time is the place where the fate of every aspect of evolution, cosmological, natural, racial and historical, will be decided. All future outcomes are at stake here and now.

Fourth and last, the urgency of the calling to chosen individuals at the present time, to participate in making this decision and shaping the outcome, by joining the organization of theosophists and coming under the guidance of the Masters, is explained.

In short, a new role for the dead, their concern with future human lives, the crisis of the present moment and the vocation of an elite are all encompassed and given a definitive form. Together, these elements create a narrative that will be expressed in pulp magazine stories and developed and adapted in response to each new circumstance in the twentieth century.

Bibliography

Ahlstrom, Sydney, *A Religious History of the American People*, New Haven, Yale University Press, 1972.
Albanese, Catherine, *A Republic of Mind and Spirit: A Cultural History of American Metaphysical Religion*, New Haven, Yale University Press, 2007.
Aldiss, Brian, *Trillion Year Spree*, London, Gollancz, 1986 [1973].
Ardener, Edwin, *The Voice of Prophecy and Other Essays*, New York, Berghahn Books, 2007.
Ashley, Mike and Robert Lowndes, *The Gernsback Days: A Study of the Evolution of Modern Science Fiction from 1911 to 1936*, Holicong, PA, Wildside Press, 2004.
Barker, A. T. (ed.), *The Mahatma Letters to A. P. Sinnett from the Mahatmas M. and K. H.*, London, T. Fisher Unwin, 1924.
Barkun, Michael, *A Culture of Conspiracy: Apocalyptic Visions in Contemporary America*, Berkeley, University of California Press, 2003.
Barrow, Logie, *Independent Spirits: Spiritualism and English Plebeians 1850–1910*, London, Routledge and Kegan Paul, 1986.
Barzun, Jacques, *Race: A Study in Modern Superstition*, New York, Harcourt, Brace and Co., 1937.
Beaty, Bart, *Fredric Wertham and the Critique of Mass Culture*, Jackson, MS, University Press of Mississippi, 2005.
Bender, Courtney, *The New Metaphysicals: Spirituality and the American Religious Imagination*, Chicago University of Chicago Press, 2010.
Bergonzi, Bernard, *The Early H. G. Wells: A Study of the Scientific Romances*, Toronto, University of Toronto Press, 1961.
Besant, Annie and C. W. Leadbeater, *Man: Whence, How and Whither*, Adyar, The Theosophical Society, 1960 [1913].
Bioy Casares, Adolfo, *The Invention of Morel*, New York, New York Review of Books, 2003 [1940; E.T. 1964].
Blavatsky, Helena Petrovna, *Isis Unveiled*, 2 vols, Boris de Zirkoff (ed.), Wheaton, IL, The Theosophical Publishing House, 1972 [1877].
Blavatsky, Helena Petrovna, *The Secret Doctrine: The Synthesis of Science, Religion, and Philosophy*, 2 vols, Pasadena, CA, Theosophical University Press, 1999 [facsimile reprint of the original edition, London, Theosophical Publishing Company, 1888].

Bowler, Peter, *The Eclipse of Darwinism: Anti-Darwinian Evolution Theories in the Decades around 1900*, Baltimore, Johns Hopkins University Press, 1992 [1983].

Braude, Ann, *Radical Spirits: Spiritualism and Women's Rights in Nineteenth-Century America*, Bloomington, Indiana University Press, 2001 [1989].

Brueggemann, Walter, *Hope within History*, Atlanta, John Knox Press, 1987.

Bulwer-Lytton, Edward, *The Coming Race (1871)*, reprint, Bishop Auckland, Cathedral Classics, Aziloth Books, 2010.

Campbell, Bruce, *Ancient Wisdom Revived: A History of the Theosophical Movement*, Berkeley, University of California Press, 1980.

Cantril, Hadley, *The Invasion from Mars: A Study in the Psychology of Panic*, New Brunswick, Transaction Publishers, 2008 [1940].

Coleman, William Emmette, 'The Sources of Madame Blavatsky's Writings', Appendix C, in Solovyov 1895.

Coulomb, Emma, *Some Account of My Intercourse with Madame Blavatsky*, London, Elliot Stock, 1885.

Cranston, Sylvia, *HPB: The Extraordinary Life and Influence of Helena Blavatsky, Founder of the Modern Theosophical Movement*, New York, G. P. Putnam's Sons, 1993.

Crowe, Michael, *The Extraterrestrial Life Debate, 1750–1900: The Idea of a Plurality of Worlds from Kant to Lowell*, Cambridge, Cambridge University Press, 1986.

Darwin, Charles, *The Descent of Man: And Selection in Relation to Sex*, London, John Murray, 1885 [1871].

Davison, Andrew, *Astrobiology and Christian Doctrine: Exploring the Implications of Life in the Universe*, Cambridge, Cambridge University Press, 2023.

Dick, Steven J., *Plurality of Worlds: The Origins of the Extraterrestrial Life Debate from Democritus to Kant*, Cambridge, Cambridge University Press, 1982.

Dick, Steven J., *The Biological Universe: The Twentieth Century Extraterrestrial Life Debate and the Limits of Science*, Cambridge, Cambridge University Press, 1996.

Elkana, Yehuda, *The Discovery of the Conservation of Energy*, London, Hutchinson Educational, 1974.

Farrell, James, *Inventing the American Way of Death*, Philadelphia, Temple University Press, 1980.

Festinger, Leon, Henry W. Riecken and Stanley Schlachter, *When Prophecy Fails*, London, Pinter and Martin, 2008 [1956].

Gauld, Alan, *The Founders of Psychical Research*, London, Routledge and Kegan Paul, 1968.

Geuss, Raymond, 'Nietzsche and Genealogy', in Raymond Geuss, *Morality, Culture, and History. Essays on German Philosophy*, Cambridge, Cambridge University Press, 1999: 1–28.

Godwin, Joscelyn, 'Blavatsky and the First Generation of Theosophy', in *Hammer and Rothstein*, 2013: 15–31.

Godwin, Joscelyn, *The Theosophical Enlightenment*, Albany, State University of New York Press, 1994.

Halperin, David, *Intimate Alien: The Hidden Story of the UFO*, Stanford, Stanford University Press, 2020.

Hammer, Olav and Mikael Rothstein (eds), *Handbook of the Theosophical Current*, Leiden, Brill, 2013.

Hanegraaff, Wouter, *New Age Religions and Western Culture: Esotericism in the Mirror of Secular Thought*, Leiden, Brill, 1996.

Harding, Susan Friend, *The Book of Jerry Falwell*, Princeton, Princeton University Press, 2000.

Harman, P. M., *Energy, Force, and Matter: The Conceptual Development of Nineteenth-Century Physics*, Cambridge, Cambridge University Press, 1982.

Haroutunian, Joseph, *Piety versus Morality: The Passing of the New England Theology*, New York, Henry Holt, 1932.

Heinlein, Robert, 'Waldo', in *Waldo and Magic, Inc.*, New York, Doubleday (Signet), 1970 [1940].

Hesse, Mary, *Forces and Fields: The Concept of Action at a Distance in the History of Physics*, New York, Dover, 2005 [1961].

Hofstadter, Richard, 'The Paranoid Style in American Politics' (1963), in Richard Hofstadter, *The Paranoid Style in American Politics*, New York, Vintage Books, 2008: 3–40.

Huxley, Aldous, *Brave New World*, London, Vintage Books, 2007 [1932].

Jacobs, David Michael, *The UFO Controversy in America*, Bloomington, Indiana University Press, 1975.

James, William, 'Presidential Address', *Proceedings of the Society for Psychical Research*, XII, December 1896.

James, William, *The Varieties of Religious Experience: A Study in Human Nature*, London, Longmans Green and Co., 1944 [1902].

Jameson, Fredric, *Archaeologies of the Future: The Desire Called Utopia and Other Science Fictions*, London, Verso, 2005.

Jenkins, Timothy, 'Fieldwork and the Perception of Everyday Life', *Man* 29(2), 1994: 433–455.

Jenkins, Timothy, *Of Flying Saucers and Social Scientists: A Re-reading of When Prophecy Fails and of Cognitive Dissonance*, New York, Palgrave Macmillan, 2013.

Johnson, Paul, *The Masters Revealed: Madame Blavatsky and the Myth of the Great White Lodge*, Albany, State University of New York Press, 1994.

Jones, Graham, *Magic's Reason: An Anthropology of Analogy*, Chicago, University of Chicago Press, 2017.
Kafton-Minkel, Walter, *Subterranean Worlds*, Port Townsend, Washington, Loompanics Unlimited, 1989.
Keel, John, 'The Man Who Invented Flying Saucers' (1986), in John Keel, *Searching for the String: Selected Writings of John H. Keel*, Andy Colvin (ed.), Point Pleasant, WV, New Saucerian Books, 2014: 117–125.
Kittler, Friedrich, *Gramophone, Film, Typewriter*, Stanford, CA, Stanford University Press, 1999 [1986].
Kripal, Jeffrey, *Mutants and Mystics: Science Fiction, Superhero Comics and the Paranormal*, Chicago, Chicago University Press, 2011.
Leadbeater, C. W., *Man Visible and Invisible*, Wheaton, IL, The Theosophical Publishing House, 1975 (abridged) [1902].
Leadbeater, C. W., *The Astral Plane*, London, Theosophical Publishing Society, 1895.
Leadbeater, C. W., *The Masters and the Path*, Chicago, Theosophical Press, 2010 [1925].
Liljegren, S. B., *Bulwer-Lytton's Novels and Isis Unveiled*, Essays and Studies on English Language and Literature XVIII, Lund, Uppsala University English Institute, 1957.
Luckhurst, Roger, *The Invention of Telepathy: 1870–1901*, Oxford, Oxford University Press, 2002.
Macintyre, Alastair, *Three Rival Versions of Moral Enquiry: Encyclopaedia, Genealogy, and Tradition*, London, Duckworth, 1990.
McLoughlin, William, *Revivals, Awakenings, and Reform*, Chicago, University of Chicago Press, 1980 [1978].
Meade, Marion, *Madame Blavatsky: The Woman Behind the Myth*, New York, G. P. Putnam's Sons, 1980.
Meerloo, Joost, *The Rape of the Mind: The Psychology of Thought Control – Menticide and Brainwashing*, New York, World Publishing Co., 1956.
Méheust, Bertrand, *Somnambulisme et médiumnité (1784–1849)*, 2 vols, Paris, Institut synthélabo pour le progrès de la connaissance, 1999.
Moore, R. Laurence, *In Search of White Crows: Spiritualism, Parapsychology, and American Culture*, New York, Oxford University Press, 1977.
Moskowitz, Sam, *The Immortal Storm: A History of Science Fiction*, Westport, CT, Hyperion, 1974.
Nethercot, Arthur H., *The First Five Lives of Annie Besant*, Chicago, University of Chicago Press, 1960.
Nethercot, Arthur H., *The Last Four Lives of Annie Besant*, Chicago, University of Chicago Press, 1963.

Noakes, Richard, *Physics and Psychics: The Occult and the Sciences in Modern Britain*, Cambridge, Cambridge University Press, 2019.
Olcott, Henry Steel, *Old Diary Leaves: The True History of the Theosophical Society*, 6 vols, Adyar, Theosophical Publishing House, 1972–1975.
Olcott, Henry Steel, *People from the Other World*, Hartford, CT, American Press, 1875.
Orwell, George, *Nineteen Eighty-Four*, London, Secker and Warburg, 1949.
Owen, Alex, *The Darkened Room: Women, Power, and Spiritualism in Late Victorian England*, Chicago, University of Chicago Press, 2004a [1989].
Owen, Alex, *The Place of Enchantment: British Occultism and the Culture of the Modern*, Chicago, University of Chicago Press, 2004b.
Packard, Vance, *The Hidden Persuaders*, Harmondsworth, Penguin Books, 1964 [1957].
Palmer, Ray, *The Secret World*, Amherst, WI, Amherst Press, 1975.
Papineau, David, *Thinking about Consciousness*, Oxford, Clarendon Press, 2002.
Partridge, Christopher (ed.), *UFO Religions*, London, Routledge, 2003.
Peebles, Curtis, *Watch the Skies! A Chronicle of the Flying Saucer Myth*, Washington, Smithsonian Institution Press, 1994.
Peters, John Durham, *Speaking into the Air: A History of the Idea of Communication*, Chicago, University of Chicago Press, 1999.
Prothero, Stephen, *The White Buddhist: The Asian Odyssey of Henry Steel Olcott*, Bloomington, IN, Indiana University Press, 2011 [1996].
Reynolds, David, *Beneath the American Renaissance*, Cambridge, MA, Harvard University Press, 1988.
Riesman, David, *The Lonely Crowd, a Study of the Changing American Character*, New Haven, Yale University Press, 2001 [1950].
Roberts, Adam, *Science Fiction*, London, Routledge, 2000.
Roberts, Adam, *The History of Science Fiction*, London, Palgrave Macmillan, 2016.
Robertson, David G., *UFOs, Conspiracy Theories and the New Age*, London, Bloomsbury, 2016.
Roth, Christopher, 'Ufology as Anthropology: Race, Extraterrestrials, and the Occult', in Debbora Battaglia (ed.), *E.T. Culture: Anthropology in Outerspaces*, Durham, Duke University Press, 2005: 38–93.
Rowell, Geoffrey, *Hell and the Victorians*, Oxford, Clarendon Press, 1974.
Rudwick, Martin, *Earth's Deep History: How It Was Discovered and Why It Matters*, Chicago, Chicago University Press, 2014.
Rupke, Nicolaas, *Richard Owen: Biology without Darwin*, Chicago, University of Chicago Press, 2009.

Scott Elliot, W., *The Story of Atlantis, and The Lost Lemuria*, London, Theosophical Publishing House, 2013 [1896; 1904].

Seed, David, *Anticipations: Essays on Early Science Fiction and Its Precursors*, Liverpool, Liverpool University Press, 1995.

Shapin, Steven, *The Scientific Life: A Moral History of a Late Modern Vocation*, Chicago, University of Chicago Press, 2008.

Shaver, Richard S., *I Remember Lemuria* (1945), reprint, LaVergne, Tennessee, 2016.

Shippey, Tom, 'Introduction', in Tom Shippey (ed.), *The Oxford Book of Science Fiction Stories*, London, Oxford University Press, 1992: ix–xiv.

Shippey, Tom, *Hard Reading: Learning from Science Fiction*, Liverpool, Liverpool University Press, 2016.

Shupe, Anson and David Bromley (eds), *The New Vigilantes: Deprogrammers, Anti-cultists, and the New Religions*, Beverley Hills, Sage, 1980.

Sinnett, A. P., *Esoteric Buddhism*, London, Theosophical Publishing House, 1972 [1883].

Sinnett, A. P., *Incidents in the Life of Madame Blavatsky, Compiled from Information Supplied by Her Relatives and Friends*, London, The Theosophical Publishing Society, 1913 [1886].

Sinnett, A. P., *The Occult World*, London, The Theosophical Publishing House, 1969 [1881].

Society for Psychical Research (Richard Hodgson's report), 'Report on Phenomena Connected with Theosophy', *Proceedings of the Society for Psychical Research*, III, December 1885.

Solovyov, Vsevolod, *A Modern Priestess of Isis*, abridged and translated by Walter Leaf, London, Longmans, Green, 1895.

Standish, David, *Hollow Earth*, Cambridge, MA, Da Capo Press, 2006.

Steinmeyer, Jim, *Hiding the Elephant: How Magicians Invented the Impossible*, London, Arrow Books, 2005.

Stocking, George, *Victorian Anthropology*, New York, The Free Press, 1987.

Suvin, Darko, *Metamorphoses of Science Fiction: On the Poetics and History of a Literary Genre*, Oxford, Peter Lang, 2016 [1979].

Taylor, Charles, *A Secular Age*, Cambridge, MA, Harvard University Press, 2007.

Taylor, Charles, *Sources of the Self: The Making of the Modern Identity*, Cambridge, Cambridge University Press, 1989.

Theobald, Morell, *Spirit Workers in the Home Circle*, London, T. Fisher Unwin, 1887.

Tillett, Gregory, *The Elder Brother: A Biography of Charles Webster Leadbeater*, London, Routledge and Kegan Paul, 1982.

Toronto, Richard, *War Over Lemuria: Richard Shaver, Ray Palmer and the Strangest Chapter of 1940s Science Fiction*, Jefferson, NC, McFarland, 2013.

Turner, Frank, *Between Science and Religion: The Reaction to Scientific Naturalism in Late Victorian England*, New Haven, Yale University Press, 1974.
Vint, Sherryl, *Science Fiction: A Guide for the Perplexed*, London, Bloomsbury, 2014.
Warner, Harry, *All Our Yesterdays: An Informal History of Science Fiction Fandom in the Forties*, Chicago, Advent Publishers, 1969.
Washington, Peter, *Madame Blavatsky's Baboon: Theosophy and the Emergence of the Western Guru*, London, Secker and Warburg, 1993.
Wells, H. G., 'The Time Machine' [1895], in *The Short Stories of H. G. Wells*, London, Ernest Benn, 1960: 9–91.
Wells, H. G., *The War of the Worlds*, Harmondsworth, Penguin Books, 1962 [1897].
Wentworth, Jim, *Giants in the Earth: The Amazing Story of Ray Palmer, Oahspe and the Shaver Mystery*, Amherst, WI: Palmer Publications, 1973.
Wertham, Fredric, *The Seduction of the Innocent*, New York, Rinehart., 1954.
Witte, Count Sergei, *The Memoirs of Count Witte*, New York, Doubleday, Page and Co., 1921.
Wittenberg, David, *Time Travel: The Popular Philosophy of Narrative*, New York, Fordham University Press, 2013.
Wolfe, Gary, *Evaporating Genres: Essays on the Fantastic*, Middletown, Wesleyan University Press, 2011.
Yates, Frances, *The Rosicrucian Enlightenment*, London, Routledge, 2002 [1972].
Young, George, *The Russian Cosmists: The Esoteric Futurism of Nikolai Fedorov and His Followers*, New York, Oxford University Press, 2012.
Young, Michael, *The Rise of the Meritocracy*, Harmondsworth, Pelican, 1967 [1958].
Zirkoff, Boris de, 'Introduction' to Blavatsky 1972.

Index

Adamski, George 79, 80
Akashic record 67, 77, 84, 110
Albanese, Catherine 2, 40, 44, 79, 140
ancient wisdom 44, 56, 64, 102, 131 *see also* Secret Doctrine
Ardener, Edwin 53, 66
Ashley, Mike 76
astral
   body 51, 107, 109, 114, 138
   other forms 61, 63, 72, 115
   plane 60, 77, 109
autodidact 15, 80, 106, 132

Barrow, Logie 16, 54, 91, 106
Bender, Courtney 2
Besant, Annie 40, 76, 77, 120, 137
Blavatsky, Helena Petrovna 33–73
Braude, Ann 45–48
Brave New World 86
Buddhism, Esoteric 99–143
Bulwer-Lytton, Edward 19, 21, 40, 56, 103

catastrophes 58, 60, 61, 64, 128, 129, 132, 133
centralization 29, 30, 89 *see also* technicians
Coming Race 19, 20, 34, 79, 96 *see also* races
communication 3, 17, 22, 29–30, 35, 45, 84, 88, 90, 94–97, 101, 112, 116, 136, 137 *see also* information
conspiracy theory 28 *see also* paranoid style

correspondences 96, 104, 107, 120, 128, 142
Cosmic Mind 53, 57, 66, 68, 77, 96, 108, 118, 122, 134, 141, 142
Cosmic or World Soul 57, 66, 70
cosmology 41, 50, 104, 116
Cranston, Sylvia 39, 42, 43, 44, 51
cycle
   human 124–128
   of life 34, 57, 108, 112, 118–120, 122, 125, 127
   planetary 118, 132
   of races 127–131, 132
   see also evolution; round

Darwin, Charles 57, 58, 60, 79, 96, 102, 116–117, 120, 121
Davis, Andrew Jackson 40, 44, 47, 48, 140
degeneration 18, 23–28, 88
descent of man 58, 59, 60, 72, 99, 102, 142
drugs 21, 28, 88, 90, 93

Earth (in the present time) 35, 36, 65, 112, 118, 122–124, 134, 143
energy 20–21, 23, 24, 27, 34, 54, 55
evolution 34, 52, 57–64, 65, 72, 79, 95–96, 99, 108, 117–118, 120–125, 127–28, 141–142 *see also* cycle of life; round

Festinger, Leon 79
Film Noir 28, 85

Gernsback, Hugo 10, 13
Great White Lodge 105 *see also* lodges

Hammer, Olav and Mikael Rothstein 3, 39, 109
Harman, P. M. 54, 55, 56
heaven 7, 46–48, 50, 110, 111–113, 142
Heinlein, Robert 24, 36
Hofstadter, Richard 90–93
Huxley, Aldous 28, 86
Huxley, Thomas 62, 63

information 22, 30, 35, 36, 67, 87–90, 93–95, 97, 136 *see also* communication
inspiration 77, 94, 104, 127, 135, 137 *see also* mind-to-mind contact; telepathy
intelligence
  artificial 10, 36, 76
  extra-terrestrial 36
  higher 57, 59, 70, 141
  mental 21, 52, 72, 126, 138
  military 27, 93
intermediate state 113
Isis Unveiled 39, 40, 44, 49, 100–104, 142

James, William 2, 51, 84, 135
Jameson, Fredric 6, 88
Jenkins, Timothy 66, 73, 79, 106

Karma 104, 108–111, 113
Keel, John 12–16, 83
Kripal, Jeffrey 3, 12–14, 19, 20, 44, 82–83, 87, 94

Leadbeater, C. W. 40, 76–77, 137
Liberal Protestant Christianity 1, 8, 45, 47, 50, 67
lodges 67, 79 *see also* Great White Lodge
Lovecraft, H. P. 80, 96, 129

malice 87, 89, 92, 93
'Mantong' 13, 86, 95
Masters 33, 39, 44, 45, 50, 67, 77, 79, 86, 95, 99, 101, 115, 125, 134, 137, 143
  Adepts 39, 51, 68, 69, 71, 73, 102, 104
  Brotherhood 44, 105–106
  Brothers 39, 51
  Mahatmas 39, 102, 103, 105, 115, 127
  see also planetary spirits
matter (cf. spirit) 24, 34, 36, 48, 52, 54–56, 61, 64, 68, 70, 75, 99, 107, 108, 118, 121–123, 125, 133, 139, 141, 142
Meade, Marion 39, 40, 42–44, 50, 51, 103
media 17, 28, 31, 43, 84, 88–91, 93
memory 5, 62, 65, 67–68, 76, 85, 85, 93, 107, 110, 120, 130, 134, 141
mental control 30 *see also* telepathy
metaphysical religion 1, 2, 42, 78
migration between planets 24–27, 87
mind-to-mind contact 84 *see also* inspiration; telepathy
Monad 65, 68, 112, 118–123, 126–128, 132, 137
Moore, R. Laurence 45
Müller, Max 79

Nethercot, Arthur 76
Newton, Sir Isaac 45, 53, 131

Olcott, Henry Steel 39, 40, 43, 44, 49, 50, 51, 101, 110, 140
Orwell, George 86
Owen, Alex 47, 137

Palmer, Ray 12–15, 62, 80, 82, 83, 87
paranoia 12, 14, 16, 28, 31, 34, 90, 93, 95, 97
paranoid style 90–92
past lives 67, 77, 110
Peters, John Durham 36, 54, 94, 136

Index   155

planetary spirits 38, 68, 69, 70, 72, 99, 142 *see also* Masters
planets 21, 23, 35, 56, 58, 65–66, 68–73, 116–127
progression 48, 116–120, 124, 128–129, 143
Prothero, Stephen 39, 44–46, 49, 50, 140
pulp magazines (subculture) 1, 8, 12, 13, 15, 76, 129, 143

races 22, 61–64, 71, 72, 78, 82–83, 122, 124, 127–131 *see also* Coming Race; cycle of life; round; root-race
radiation 21, 23–29, 34, 56, 82, 88, 95
rays 21–28, 29, 31, 81–85, 88, 89, 94–96
Reformation 6–7
reform movements 37, 45–48, 49–50, 106
reincarnation 102, 104, 105, 109, 114
relay 38, 48, 52, 99 *see also* spirits
religion
    Indian 79
    Judeo-Christian 1–2, 9, 46–48, 50, 79, 100–101, 111, 113, 141, 142
Roberts, Adam 6–9
root-race 63, 127–131 *see also* races
Roth, Christopher 3, 78–80, 81, 83, 90
round 62–63, 119, 124–127, 128, 138 *see also* cycle of life; evolution
Rowell, Geoffrey 113–114, 117

scale 3, 12, 34, 37, 52–54, 56, 60, 99, 121, 128, 131, 133, 136, 142
Schopenhauer, Arthur 89
science fiction 4–6, 6–11, 36 *see also* pulp magazines
second order categories 37
Secret Doctrine, The 39, 40, 52–73, 99, 100, 102, 104, 129

Secret Doctrine 84, 123 *see also* ancient wisdom
secret history 19, 28–32
secret societies 37, 79, 92, 100, 106
secrets 19, 22, 30, 33–34, 44, 51, 87, 106
septenary principle 69, 102, 107, 128
Shaver Mystery 11–16, 76–97
Shaver, Richard 3–32, 75–97
Shippey, Tom 6, 86
Sinnett, Alfred 40, 42, 50–51, 77, 100–143
sixth sense 56, 67, 137–140
solar system 34, 57, 71, 117, 141–142
Solovyov, Vsevolod 40, 42, 52
soul 48, 65, 72, 107–112, 116, 126, 127, 133, 138
spirit (cf. matter) 4, 20, 48, 65, 68, 70, 108–114, 117–123, 126–127, 135–137, 139
spirits 3, 19, 52–53, 57, 58, 65, 68–72, 77, 99–100 *see also* Monad; planetary spirit; relay; soul
spiritualism 6, 37–39, 41–44, 45–50, 100–102, 114–116, 137
subterranean world 17, 18, 19–20, 24, 80
Suvin, Darko 5, 6, 88
Swedenborg 40, 48, 57, 71, 140

technicians 20–30, 87–90 *see also* centralization
teleology 38
telepathy 35, 36, 94, 127 *see also* inspiration; mental control
theodicy 16–17, 37, 53, 67, 76, 82, 104–105, 107–114, 116, 128, 132, 135, 136, 139, 140
Theosophical Society 39, 44, 51, 76
Theosophy
    relation to religion (western and eastern) 100–101, 140–143

relation to scientific discoveries 52–73
relation to Spiritualism 41–52
Tillett, Gregory 77
time travel 7, 66, 75, 84–86, 126
Toronto, Richard 13–16, 81
travel between planets 7, 34, 35, 37, 65, 123

Vint, Sherryl 9–11

vitalism 17, 18, 20–22, 23, 78, 79
vocation 65, 84, 95–97, 127, 143

Wells, H. G. 8, 80, 86
Wentworth, Jim 13, 14, 83
Williamson, George Hunt 79, 80
Wittenberg, David 67, 84–86

Zirkoff, Boris de 40, 49, 101–103

Mini Series: Images of Elsewhere
TIMOTHY JENKINS

Vol. I
Flying Saucers: An Introduction

Vol. II
Religion and Science Fiction

Vol. III
Martian Linguistics

Vol. IV
UFO Reports

Vol. V
Alien Sightings

Vol. VI
Images of Elsewhere

www.ingramcontent.com/pod-product-compliance
Ingram Content Group UK Ltd.
Pitfield, Milton Keynes, MK11 3LW, UK
UKHW021323180426
11947UKWH00017B/1404